THE HOUSE ON THE MOUNTAIN

THE HOUSE ON THE MOUNTAIN

HELEN MCCABE

THORNDIKE
CHIVERS

This Large Print edition is published by Thorndike Press, Waterville, Maine, USA and by AudioGO Ltd, Bath, England.
Thorndike Press, a part of Gale, Cengage Learning.
Copyright © 2010 by Helen McCabe.
The moral right of the author has been asserted.

LIBRARY OF CONGRESS CATALOGING-IN-PUBLICATION DATA

McCabe, Helen, 1942–
    The house on the mountain / by Helen McCabe. — Large print ed.
        p. cm. — (Thorndike Press large print gentle romance)
    Originally published: [S.l.] : Sutal Ltd., 2010.
    ISBN-13: 978-1-4104-3753-2
    ISBN-10: 1-4104-3753-1
    1. Large type books. I. Title.
    PR6113.C35H68 2011
    823'.92—dc22   2011005512

BRITISH LIBRARY CATALOGUING-IN-PUBLICATION DATA AVAILABLE

Published in 2011 by arrangement with Sutal Ltd, Management & Production.
Published in 2011 in the U.K. by arrangement with the author.

U.K. Hardcover: 978 1 445 83664 5 (Chivers Large Print)
U.K. Softcover: 978 1 445 83665 2 (Camden Large Print)

Printed in the United States of America   i
1 2 3 4 5 6 7 15 14 13 12 11

THE HOUSE ON THE MOUNTAIN

CHAPTER 1

'I know it's nothing to do with me,' said June, 'but are you sure you're going to be all right?'

'What are you worried about, June? Do you think I shouldn't go or something?' Ella smiled, thinking that ever since she'd been taken on as a paying guest at the villa, she had never seen June less than optimistic. This was a first. Ella might have envied June's view on life, if she hadn't been so happy with her own at the moment, doing a job she loved on a beautiful Greek island.

'It's an awful road at night,' replied June. 'I hate those hairpin bends and I've been driving round here for ages — and you know what Greek drivers are like,' she grimaced.

'I know, but are you saying I've become as crazy as that?' joked Ella. 'Sorry . . .' She caught the other's expression. 'I can see you're worried, but you know *I* don't drive like that. I'll be careful.'

'I expect you think I sound just like your mother,' June replied. Ella smiled.

'You're not in the least like her.' Ella's mind flicked to her mother, an elegant woman who had hosted many dinners so expertly when her parents had been in the Diplomatic Service; who had known exactly the right thing to say on every occasion and always knew the right thing to wear. The Embassy had been extremely popular when her parents had been there. To Ella, her mother seemed utterly English and extraordinarily conventional, whereas June, although about the same age, was a free spirit and entirely unconventional. She had married a Greek and had settled near Rhodes Town. When her husband died, she had decided not to go back to England. Privately, and from what Ella had gleaned, June was a kind of Shirley Valentine, who couldn't bear to leave the island of her dreams.

Ella could see why Dimitri had fallen for June. Not only had she a motherly nature, but also a fiery one. She spoke as she found, wore what she liked and cared little for anyone's good opinion. That evening, she was dressed in a floaty, aquamarine caftan and her long dark hair which had not lost its thickness, but was streaked with grey in places, fell below her shoulders. She was also sporting two of the largest gold hooped earrings Ella had ever seen. Added to that, the rest of her gold jewellery clinked when she moved her arms, tanned a deep walnut brown. To look at her, one could hardly believe she wasn't a Greek. However at that moment, she still had an anxious look.

Ella put her hand on June's arm. 'You don't have to worry about me. Remember I almost grew up here.'

'But you weren't driving then! You were only ten.' They both laughed, breaking the tension. 'Take no notice of me, but you be careful.'

'I always am. Trust me.' She was

used to the mountain road now and she would take care. What else could she do in her little car anyway? It only chugged along. It was not as if she was driving a Ferrari!

'I'll go and make a cup of tea.' June had never given up her fondness for English tea.

'Lovely,' murmured Ella, as she watched her landlady make her way towards the kitchen. She couldn't have been happier since she had taken the upper part of the villa. June had needed a paying guest to keep the old place in the manner to which it had once been accustomed. It had been in her husband, Dimitri's family for many years, but he and June had never had any children and the younger members of his family were now living in brand new houses on the other side of town. Now, the villa was lonely for young company, its once-white outer walls dreaming of a re-paint, but inside it was still a haven of quiet colours, which reflected the never-ending sunny days of blue skies and sea. Yes, the Villa Agios, like its owner had welcomed Ella with open arms.

After Ella had finished her cup of tea which had been complemented with at least two of June's honey cakes, she said, 'Don't ask me to have any more, June, or I shan't be able to cram in any of that lovely roast lamb I'm going to get at the festival. I'll go and get ready now.'

She ran up to the top floor, which was in her opinion the most beautiful part of the house. She occupied a large bedroom with the luxury of a pale-blue tiled en-suite and had what was once a smaller bedroom, as a living room, where she could sit on the terrace, and look out to sea across towards the harbour. 'Oh, dear,' she said out loud as she saw the books and papers strewn across the table. 'You don't look like the organised teacher you think you are. No, Ella, I think you'll have to start clearing up soon.' But then as she strayed outside to be rewarded by the sight of the sun dipping into the sea, illuminating everything in a gold light, she thought, Why am I bothering with tidying up when I have a view like this?

In the distance, across the jumble of masts belonging to yachts and fishing boats, a massive cruise liner was tethered, almost dwarfing the old town walls. She imagined the press of tourists thronging the streets on the look out for bargains which were for sale everywhere in the pretty streets of the Old Town. She had loved Rhodes ever since she and her parents had taken all their vacations there. Her father had been posted to Athens for several years and as a classicist had a great fondness for the Greek Islands, which he had passed on to his only daughter, regaling her with the old tales and myths of gods and goddesses.

Ella was fortunate that she spoke excellent Greek, which had been of the greatest advantage when she landed the job as an English teacher in Rhodes. But she hadn't wanted to teach at Secondary Level on the island. No, she was more interested

14

in working with small children and when the agency had advertised the post of working as an assistant teacher at the *dimotiko* in the little village in the mountains outside Rhodes, she had applied for it even though she was over qualified for a primary. Strangely enough, it was the village where June's husband had been born and June knew practically everyone around there. She had been useful for filling in any blank spaces needed re village life!

The job was turning out to be exactly what Ella wanted. According to June, the governors had "known a good thing when they saw it" and appointed her. She had already completed one term until the school broke up at the end of May and Ella felt she had begun to be accepted by her pupils and their parents. But now the summer was here and next term did not start until September. So Ella was prepared to enjoy herself and take advantage of the holidays by soaking in the days of sun and sea. That night she was determined to attend the festival which was taking place in the village to mark their Saint's Day. According to Takis, who was one of the governors, it was a night not to be missed. He had even offered to fetch her, but she'd declined. Charming though he was, somehow she didn't want to make a professional relationship into something more personal. She had known he was interested in her ever since she had arrived. But Ella was less than keen and spent some time dodging his slowly-increasing advances.

Ella turned from the view and started to go through her wardrobe. She had to strike a balance between being the serious teacher and the fun-loving girl she was underneath. She thought the Greeks took teaching as a profession more seriously than was done so in England. Ella had been surprised to find that if you carried a card saying you were a teacher you could enter all the archaeological sites free. But then the Greeks *had* been civilised since ancient times!

She settled upon a pretty, white tiered skirt and top to match. She also pulled out a shrug to put on over the halter neck. She suspected that the festival would begin or end up at the church and it would have been viewed as entirely disrespectful if a *teacher* had entered the lovely Byzantine building dressed like a tourist who didn't know better. Luckily, Ella was aware of the culture of the island having spent so much time there in the past. The villa she'd stayed in during those seemingly never-ending summers of her childhood had been a little like June's and Ella was pretty sure that was why she'd decided to room there — only temporarily of course, as she dreamed of buying a small place with her own money. Her parents had offered a sizeable deposit to set her up, but Ella had wanted to prove that she could do it all by herself in her first real job. Which she would!

She stood, brushing her long hair and stared at herself in the full-length mirror. The shrug was sweet and she was fairly satisfied with how she looked. Her mother was blonde and her father had dark hair — what remained of it — but Ella's resembled neither of her parents. Hers was tawny with glinting golden highlights. As she brushed it, she decided that she almost looked Greek given that her skin tanned easily and the summer sun had done its work by burnishing it even more in the few hot weeks she'd been in Rhodes.

She sat down and put on her sandals. At first she had decided to wear her platforms, but then she had visions of tripping down one of the flights of stone steps that abounded in the village. She discarded them and brought out another pair, golden sandals which laced above the ankle, goddess-like. She probably wouldn't be able to drive in them though! But she did keep a sensible pair of flatties for the car.

She smiled, thinking that she certainly didn't want to end up going over the side on one of the hair-raising hairpins and fulfil June's prophecy of her foolishness! She also grabbed a sweater as an after thought. The wind could whistle keenly on the top of the mountain and she suspected she was going to be very late getting home. She would leave the woolly in the car, together with her sensible shoes.

She didn't take too long over her make-up, only a moisturiser and a dusting of gold on her cheekbones, as well as a small amount of soft and dusky eye shadow and lip gloss. She preferred 'the natural look'. As she came down the open staircase, June was carrying a tray into the kitchen — and stopped. 'You look lovely,' she said.

'Thank you, June — and don't worry, I'm not going to drive in these!'

'Glad to hear it,' said June, staring at her sandals. 'You'll be late back, I assume?'

'Probably. And I'll remember about the hairpins.' They laughed out loud.

Ten minutes later, Ella was heading for the mountains. She soon turned off the coast road towards the island's interior. The view had changed from the glittering sheen of the setting sun upon the sea, to the hazy, dark outlines of the mountain range beyond, but where the last rays of the sun were striking several mountain slopes outlining the deep green patches, which Ella recognised as groves of olive trees. Harvesting the olives on such steep slopes was an art which the villagers had practised since the island was young. The lowering mountains, although stark, had a majesty the coast lacked.

Ella's little white car chugged its way up into the foothills and the tinder-dry expanses of the pine forests. When she had bought the vehicle she had been unsure of its capacity to make the long drive every day, but June had enlisted the help of a friend to buy Ella a suitable vehicle. The friend in question had an abundance of curly hair and a striking smile that displayed a wonderful set of white teeth. He had spoken in rapid Greek that Ella couldn't follow and the vendor had responded in the excited but agonised tones of a man born to haggle. They had both lain down under the vehicle and both emerged seemingly satisfied.

"A good work horse," June's friend had proclaimed and Ella bought the little car, which she had named Hermie! So her car had been named for Hermes, the fleet messenger of the gods and though, not as speedy, had proved June's friend right — so far. Although Hermie was complaining all the time as it climbed towards the village, it also had a nimble but volatile way of negotiating the famous hairpins. As the steep road finally flattened out, she could see the fairy lights, strung out along the streets, the upper ones clinging precariously to the mountain side. It was very strange, as in the day time, the mountains behind the village were very different from the ones, which she had just driven through. Their peaks were devoid of trees, except for several small forests clinging to their feet. Their great bodies were brown-pink, sheer and barren, some rising to sharp peaks, others sweeping gracefully down. Between those patches of forest, small vineyards clung precariously, making the most of a sun that poured on to them all day long. It made Ella shiver to think of going up there at night, but she could imagine the strong wind blowing and the sight of the small white village, lit up and nestling at their special mountain's feet, not fearful, but protected.

However remote, the village festival was well attended. She drove in between the lines of cars very carefully, looking for a parking space, but as she was wondering what she should do if she couldn't find anywhere to park, someone tapped on the window. 'Takis,' she said. He was smiling that soft smile with which young Greeks so easily charm women.

'This way,' he beckoned. 'I have saved you a space.'

'Thank you,' she said, about to wind the window up again, but he had his hand on it.

'Nothing but the best for our teacher.' He wore an even cheesier smile, but she didn't mind as she didn't have to worry about backing Hermie down the road again. A moment later, she was squeezing into the space. She pulled the key out of the ignition and, opening the door, was very conscious of his approving eyes.

'Well done. You almost drive like a Greek.' Privately, she thought it wasn't a compliment.

'Thank you. It was very nice of you to keep a space for me,' she said.

'I am nice,' he joked and she wondered momentarily if he was going to keep chatting her up all evening, knowing she didn't really want him to! In fact, she wasn't keen on embarking on any kind of relationship at present. She'd had her moments, but just now she wanted to please herself and enjoy her job.

As they approached the building, she felt a thrill of pleasure. The school looked so beautiful, transformed from its day-to-day self into a romantic venue. The children's tables had been brought out into the open and laid with the purest of white embroidered cloths. Flowers were abundant and the vines that wreathed about the roof dangled down. Candles glowed in the early dusk and from everywhere came the sound of laughter and music. And what was more, Ella's hungry stomach caught the delicious aroma of roasting lamb.

'Come,' said Takis, 'there are some people I would like you to meet.' She felt him slip his hand under her arm. She did not protest at his closeness, because the enchanted scene was drawing her in. A moment later, Ella was letting a smiling Takis lead her into the welcoming throng.

CHAPTER 2

Ella looked at her watch. She hadn't realised how late it was. Not that it mattered. But she had to admit she was tired and she was facing the long drive home. She had spent much of the night holding her hand over her glass as she was offered more and more wine. It would have been very easy to do as Takis suggested and stay over at his parents' house, which was very large, seeing that his family was one of the wealthiest in the area. But she knew she would have felt compromised. After all, she was not his girl friend and this was not England. She had even felt awkward being introduced to his mother and father.

Luckily, she had many other people to see and talk to, including the rest of the school governors, most of whom had interviewed her for the post. But she could feel Takis' eyes on her all the time and especially when she, together with the whole village, walked in procession to the church.

The whitewashed, red-roofed building was a delight. It stood lower than the road in its own small grounds. That special evening the bell was working overtime as it proclaimed its Saint's feast to the rest of the island.

Inside, it was sumptuous, belying its simple exterior. As the procession crowded in, Ella stood with the reverent congregation as they tasted the oil and bread. The singing was breathtaking and the candle lights flickered in front of the Saint's shrine, while the lazy perfume of incense filled the air. From the roof swung magnificent chandeliers ablaze with light. The congregation stood throughout the service as only the old and infirm were encouraged to sit.

When the rituals were over, Ella emerged into the cool island night. She felt a hand adjust the shrug. 'It's all right, Takis,' she said, withdrawing. 'I'm not cold.' He smiled, his handsome face outlined in the moonlight. Ella thought quickly how easy it would be to be taken in by this charming man, but she was sensible.

'I have to go now,' she said, 'it's late.'

'Are you sure you won't stay? You're very welcome.'

'I know that,' she said, 'but June will be worried.'

'Ah, June,' he said. 'One day you will leave her protection.' He laughed. Ella felt a trifle angry. What did he know about the relationship she had with June?

'I don't need protecting,' she said.

'I could take you home,' he offered. 'You could leave your car here and then I would return and you could pick it up on Monday.'

'No, thank you, Takis,' she replied firmly. 'I have things to do.' She was glad he didn't press her as to what they were. She hadn't the slightest idea, but one thing she was sure of — she didn't want Takis tagging along.

'It's a bad road in the dark,' he said.
'I know it now. Thank you again.'
She reversed out of the parking space.

'Be careful.' His warning irritated
her. He was treating her as if she was
his possession. Unfortunately, it
would not be good for her career to
be rude to him. He was after all the
Chairman of the school governors
and she wanted to keep him onside.

'Of course I will,' she said sweetly.
Her head was full of the delightful
evening as she manoeuvred her way
past the cars of the last stragglers.
Several children waved to her as she
passed. She thought how different it
was from England. The children were
out with their parents at all hours and
did not seem in the least worse for it.
She waved back, knowing she'd made
a good impression that evening. Ev-

eryone had wanted to talk to her and discuss how well their child had been doing. She felt she was making a difference already and that her decision to teach had been the right one. At that moment, everything in Ella's life felt rosy.

Hermie wanted to go faster, but Ella held the little car in check as she began to negotiate the steep incline. It had been bad enough going up, but then it had been light and although she'd felt very brave when she left, it was a strange feeling driving between the tall trees and knowing that on the opposite side of the road was a black nothingness. Occasionally, she caught a glimpse of twinkling lights below as she descended.

She was about half way down travelling slowly, when she saw a glimmer of headlights. Although she was being careful, the approaching driver was not. He was on her before she knew it and dazzled her by the headlights as they swung around the bend. She braked, but too late. As the car shot by, it caught Hermie with a forceful blow that spun the little car around. The only thing that Ella remembered afterwards was her momentary thankfulness that she was not driving on the left hand side, otherwise she would have gone right over the precipice. In fact, all that happened was Herbie shot down a hollow on the other side of the road and ended up on its side in a little clearing.

Ella could smell petrol as she came to. She panicked then, trying to get out of her seatbelt, but she couldn't undo it in the dark. The seconds that followed were the most frightening Ella had ever experienced. She was afraid Hermie was going to set on fire, trapping her inside. She had no time even to pray as she felt the driver's door being wrenched open and a powerful torch shining on her.

'Help me,' she cried.

'Don't worry!' It was only afterwards that she realised the man had spoken in English. She could feel his hands searching to open the seat belt and then — she was free. Next moment she felt him dragging her away from the car and up the slope. At the top, she collapsed in a crumpled heap, while the torch searched her body.

'Where are you hurt?' he asked.

'I don't know,' she sobbed.

'Don't panic. You're speaking. You're all right.' She felt his hands on her. 'You're lucky.' She didn't feel it! Then, bending down he picked her up as if it was the easiest thing in the world. She just hung limply, her head against his shoulder as he carried her. She didn't protest as she was only conscious of his warmth bringing back the life to her shivering frame. The man strode on and soon she realised he was stooping to go through a low lintel.

She blinked as the light dazzled her eyes. Then she felt herself being put down gently on to a couch. Ella looked round and with relief realised she was in a comfortable living room. She remembered then that she was still clinging to him and feeling rather foolish, let go of his neck and tried to stand up.

'No. Don't try it! Lie flat for a moment. You might be in shock. Do you hurt anywhere else?' he repeated, his hands checking her limbs.

'No, I just ache all over. How did you find me?' She sat up, then sank back again, feeling weak.

'I heard the bang,' he replied grimly. Her eyes focused on him.

'You speak English,' she said, then realised she ought to be thanking him again. 'Is the car all right?' He stood back.

'I doubt it,' he said, 'but it's only a lump of metal. You're the one who matters.' She could see him properly now. He was lean and tall, wearing a black jacket with a yellow-green flash over a pair of jeans. But what she noticed most was the expression on his face, as if he was as scared as she was.

'Are you a policeman?' He ignored the question.

'I shouldn't have moved you,' he said, 'but the car might have gone on fire.' It was as if he was blaming himself. 'I ought to get you checked out at the hospital, but seeing as we're up a mountain at midnight that's not a possibility at present. How do you feel?'

Ella realised her teeth were chattering. 'All right.'

'You don't look it. Probably the shock. You were very lucky!' He walked across the room and returned with a blanket. A moment later, he was wrapping it round her. 'Now just lie there until you calm down.' She tried to get up then. 'What are you doing?'

'I need to make a phone call. Where's my handbag?' A moment of panic overtook her. Perhaps he'd picked it up?

'Here it is. It's quite safe.' She could see by his expression that he knew what she was thinking.

'Thank you.' She rummaged in it, searching for her mobile.

'Not now,' he said. 'Just calm down. I suggest you shut your eyes. Anyway, you won't get a signal here. Too many trees. When you feel better you can call who you like.'

'I really ought to go home.' He regarded her and she could see that he was irritated.

'Sorry,' he said. 'You're stuck with me right now.'

'Have you a car?'

'I have a truck out there and it's staying there. You're going nowhere and neither am I.' She felt panicky again. 'Don't worry, I'm not going to hurt you. I've just saved your life, remember!' All at once, she felt stupid and childish. 'By the way, I'm Loukas. I'm quite safe. And I used to be a fireman.' He held out his hand.

'I'm Ella — and I'm a teacher.' She shook hands with him, wondering if he could feel her shaking.

'Let's hope you're a better teacher than you're a driver,' he said. 'That's a bad bend. How could you have been so stupid to drive around here at this time of night — and on a dangerous road like this?'

'I beg your pardon,' she said, offended. Who was he calling stupid? 'It was that idiot coming up,' she

snapped. She didn't like being patro-
nised.

'We Greeks are pretty good drivers.
It's the ones we hit who are the
problem.' He grinned, his mood
changing like quicksilver. 'Well, you
seem all right. Except for shaking!'

'I'm fine,' she snapped again, not
joining in the joke. She looked round.
'June will be anxious about me.' She
tried to get up again.

'June will understand. You can use
the phone here, now I know you're
all right. Sorry, I can't bring it over.
It's a bit old-fashioned.' Her legs
were still shaking. A second later, he
was steadying her. 'Careful.' It was
just hitting her what might have happened. 'You can sit down while you
use it.'

He brought over a chair, white and

very pretty like one from a taverna. As she picked up the receiver she noted other things in the room that displayed a woman's touch. A delicate wall-hanging. Flowers under a photograph. Where was his girl friend? Or even his wife? By now, she was taking in the contents of this very comfortable room. Through an archway, she could see a modern kitchen and a large table surrounded by more white taverna chairs. Suddenly she felt safe — and much happier.

CHAPTER 3

She used the touch button phone
with trembling fingers. 'June? It's
Ella. Yes . . . I'm sorry you were worried. But I've . . . had an accident. . . .
No, nothing serious, but the car's not
driveable. Yes, I am safe. I'm at a
house on the mountain. At Mr. . . . ?'
She looked across at him.

'Milas. Loukas Milas.'

'Mr. Milas'. I'm with Loukas Milas . . . Yes, that's right. He rescued
me from the car — and I'm very
grateful.' She watched Loukas walk
away and begin to take down two

glasses from a large, dark, wooden dresser. 'No. I can't get home. I'm staying here. Of course, I'll be all right. Why shouldn't I be? I'll be back as soon as possible in the morning. Don't worry about me, please, June. 'Night.' She put down the handset.

'She's a nice lady,' said Loukas, pouring at a drink. 'Here, this will do you good.'

'Is it alcohol?' He shook his head. 'Do you know June then. The Villa Agios?'

'Yes.' She felt relieved. 'Come and sit down over here.' He gestured towards a comfortable-looking couch with soft multi-coloured cushions. She shook her head.

'I'll just sit here for a moment.' She hoped she didn't sound suspicious of his motives.

'Then I suggest you go to bed. You look as if you need to.' She felt herself relaxing, although she was conscious of tension between them. He was being civil now, but she had the feeling he didn't want her to be there. I'm probably cramping his style, she thought. Her mind was summing up all kinds of possibilities. Perhaps he was worried that the mythical girl friend/wife wouldn't take kindly to finding another woman in the house. Or maybe it was his mother? But he didn't look as if he lived with his mother.

'You find me interesting?' he asked. Ella wasn't given to blushing, but she could feel the colour rising in her face.

'I'm sorry,' she said, 'but I think I should go and lie down like you said.'

She looked round feeling very shaky, but what she'd had to drink had left a warm feeling in her stomach. Then she was assailed with another moment of panic. What if he'd spiked it? Oh, no he wouldn't, she told herself. 'Where do I go?'

'Come,' he said. A moment later, he was walking through the arch and across to another doorway, which revealed a flight of stone steps. It was then she almost fell over a toy truck. 'I'm sorry,' he said, picking it up and offering his arm.

'It's okay. I'm fine,' she said. He withdrew the offer and went on ahead towards the steps. She felt relieved. If there was a child somewhere in this, then she should be all right. She climbed the flight behind him and he opened a door which led into a dark room. He switched on the light and went across to pull down the shutters. The walls were a dusky pink owing to the shades of the two bedside lamps. She was surprised at the bedroom's femininity.

'You'll be able to see the view in the morning from the balcony. My . . . I mean . . . people call it spectacular.' He was retreating towards the door. 'The bathroom is next door. It's okay. I have an en suite.' She caught her breath. 'Just wait there and I shall bring you some towels.' She collapsed on to the bed and waited. A moment later he returned with a carefully-folded armful. 'I hope these will do. They haven't been used for ages.'

'They look great,' she said. She knew she was right now. Loukas must have a woman in tow, because no way would he be using white embroidered towels. Nor would he backtrack when he was about to say someone's name. It was evidently painful to remember her.

'Well, good night,' he said. 'Oh, and in the bathroom cabinet you will find several unused toothbrushes. There is a carafe of fresh water and a glass there. And one of my shirts! But it will be too big.' He was looking at her body.

'Thank you,' she said weakly. The man was full of surprises. Well, at least, June knew him and vice versa. He couldn't be a mad axeman! 'Good night — Ella.' The way he said her name in Greek was musical.

'It is short for Elena?' he queried.

'In England, it's just Ella.' He was

looking at her in a strange way. Almost sad.

'As I said, you were very stupid to drive down this road at night. Anything might have happened to you. *I know.*'

'Yes, I've gathered that,' she replied. She felt she could have done without the parting shot, but then she was sorry. 'Good night.' He nodded.

'Good night. And . . . I am sorry for being rude.' A moment later, he was closing the door behind him. She heard his feet pad away on the tiles, then halt. Afterwards, she heard a door closing — she relaxed — then opening again, then closing. Then — nothing.

Well, at least he apologised, she said to herself and breathed in deeply surveying her new surroundings. A beautiful wall-hanging in the same dusky pink adorned the wall. Definitely traditional. Above a chest of drawers were rows of white bookcases filled with volumes, the spines splashing colour on to the walls. She walked over and picked one up. 'Greek Language and Literature', and it wasn't a guide book. More like a university text. Whoever owned this room had been very well-educated. The others were much the same — certainly not holiday reading. She put back a book entitled 'Mythical Greece' and went over the double bed. It was immaculate. She fingered the sheets. They were pristine and the hems were worked in a traditional Greek pattern. The bedspread was of a quilted silk material in the same dusky pink. Everything pointed to the fact that this room was, or had been a woman's. And certainly not his mother's, because when Ella couldn't hold back her curiosity and opened the doors of one of the two big wardrobes, she discovered a quantity of dainty clothes carefully placed on hangers; halter tops, bikinis and pretty dresses. She could smell expensive perfume lingering, but also a sweet mustiness, making her think these clothes had not been worn for ages. Maybe she left him, thought Ella.

When she was sure he must have gone to bed, she tiptoed out of the room into the modern bathroom, which was perfectly kept. She felt bruised and sore. In the corner stood a large Greek pot in which a lovely dwarf tree, was flowering. She locked the door behind her and began to get ready for bed. She stared at his shirt. Again white and perfectly ironed. But frayed at the cuffs. She picked it up and put it on. It came to halfway down her legs! He was right. It *was* too big!

Once she'd returned to her room, she lay with her arms above her head. It was then she began to feel strangely dizzy. Thank goodness, the accident wasn't worse, she thought. I'm bound to feel like this. Her eyelids drooped and very soon Ella was asleep.

As the morning light crept in through the shutters, Ella woke up suddenly. Her sleep had been heavy but punctuated by the strangest dreams. She could hardly remember them already except two faces kept merging into her fanciful brain. One was Takis, the other Loukas. She couldn't imagine why! She hardly knew her rescuer.

Ella shook her head and roused herself up from the pillow, then held her breath. Her door was slowly opening! She drew the bedclothes around her and stared. What was she going to do? She had visions of having to throw the carafe of water at him!

A moment later, she gasped. A roguish little face was staring at her, which broke into an enchanting grin. It was followed by a small form dressed in brightly-coloured pyjamas. The little boy of about five or six hovered, clinging on to the door handle. Ella sat up. Of course, mystery solved. This was the reason why Loukas wouldn't take her straight back. He couldn't leave the child on his own. Which was a good sign.

'Hello,' she said. 'What's *your* name?' He advanced a little further. His eyes were so dark and beautiful they made her gasp. Exactly like his father's!

'Costas Milas,' he said. 'What are you doing in Mummy's room?' His smile had disappeared.

'I'm Ella,' she replied, not knowing how to answer the question. Then the awkward moment was gone. He was grinning again.

'Wait a minute.' He put up a little hand. She was so glad that she could converse in Greek with this lovely little boy. A moment later, he disappeared only to re-appear with an armful of toys and a book. 'Can we read this?'

'Of course,' she said. In a few seconds he had climbed on to the bed. They were almost halfway through when she heard a light knock. Costas looked at her and slipped off silently. He was staring at the door uncertainly. 'Come in,' she called.

Loukas appeared. Costas ran over to him and slipped his hand into his father's. 'You have met my son, then?' he said.

'Yes — and he's enchanting. We've read most of this, haven't we, Costas?' Ella said.

'He likes stories.' Loukas smiled.

'So do I,' she replied, smiling at both of them.

'Are you a teacher? Like my mummy?' asked Costas.

Ella caught the look on Loukas' face. It was like a dark cloud descend-

ing and his lips were set in a hard
line.

'Enough questions, Costas.' Loukas
turned to her. 'I'm sorry if he's
bothered you. He always wakes up
early.'

'Not at all,' she said. 'I understand.
He's lovely.'

'Sometimes,' replied Loukas, grimacing. 'Costas, go and get your slip-
pers. Then downstairs. By the way,
Ella, you speak very good Greek.'
Then he turned and disappeared,
with his son scampering in tow.

'Phew,' said Ella, leaning back
against the pillows. A few minutes
later, she was up and getting dressed.
Then she went over to the window
and, opening the shutters, let the
early morning sun fill the room with
warmth. Going out on the balcony,

she gasped at the scene. Through the wide aisles of forest trees, she could see all the way down the mountain, which on that side was a sheer drop. In the far distance a village with a jigsaw of tiny red roofs tumbled crazily down to an indigo sea. The beauty of it all overwhelmed Ella, but then she remembered where she was.

All at once, she heard his voice from the bottom of the steps. 'I have breakfast ready.' Her stomach gave a little flip and it wasn't from hunger. Running lightly down the steps she arrived in the living room to see Costas seated on a tall stool eating his breakfast, while his dark and handsome father tended to the pan. 'Omelette all right?' he asked.

'Wonderful,' she said.

'Sit down then.' He gestured towards a chair. 'Sorry, but Costas has started. He couldn't wait.'

'I can understand that too,' she said, the aroma filling her nostrils.

'Don't hold your breath. I'm not that good a cook. But my chickens are to be trusted.' At that moment, she was dying to ask Loukas if he'd been cooking for himself very long, but sense prevailed. 'Here's your omelette. Please start. I have had my breakfast.' She picked up her fork.

'Your chickens would be very happy,' she joked after the first bite. 'You're an extremely good cook,' she said.

'I try,' he answered, but she could see he was pleased with the compliment. 'Once again, I'm sorry I was so brusque last night.'

'Were you? I think I was too upset

to notice. Thank you too for what you did. I don't know what I would have done if you hadn't been around.'

'I am always around,' he said. 'Bread?' He offered her a crusty roll.

'Oh, no, I have enough with this.' All the time they were speaking, Costas had been smiling and tucking in to his breakfast. 'And then I have to go.'

'I don't want you to,' said Costas suddenly, his wide eyes fixing her over the rim of his bowl.

'You seem to have made a hit with him,' said Loukas. 'You like children.' She could see it was not a question.

'Well, I am a teacher,' she smiled. 'But that doesn't always follow!'

'You're the new teacher then?'

'Yes, in the village. You weren't at

the festival.' Neither was that a question.

'I had no one to look after Costas.'

'What a pity. It was a very good night. But . . . I think if I'd known what was going to happen, I probably wouldn't have come, and . . .' Ella knew this was her chance to ask about why he was alone, but the moment passed. But just as she was about to go on and ask him if Costas had been ill, because she had never seen him at the school, he interrupted.

'That would have been a pity also,' he said. She wasn't sure what he meant and felt a little uncomfortable again. '. . . If you had not gone to our festival. I shall take you home as soon as possible.' He looked at his watch. 'But we must wait a few minutes.' A moment later, there was a light knock on the door followed by it being pushed open. Evidently the caller was familiar.

'Ah. Anna,' he said. Ella didn't know why, but her stomach turned over. The girl halted in the doorway. She was very good-looking in a Greek way, dark curly hair, beautifully tanned, great figure and was wearing a skimpy top, shorts and sandals. She looked across at Ella, who felt the girl's eyes boring into her and immediately recognised hostility. Was this his current girl friend? No wonder she looked put out finding another woman at the house so early in the morning. She didn't speak, but walked across the room and took an apron from behind a door. She put it on, still without speaking. She was evidently trying to be rude ignoring Ella, as Greeks are well known for their hospitality.

'Anna, this is Ella. She was an unexpected guest last night. Did you see the state her car's in?'

'Yes. Is she such a bad driver?' Anna laughed.

'No, I'm afraid I was forced off the road,' retorted Ella in perfect Greek. The girl raised her eyebrows. 'By a Greek driver.' She couldn't help it.

'Ella is the new school teacher,' explained Loukas. 'She was at the festival last night.'

'Our wine is strong,' said Anna cattily, starting to clear the dishes from the breakfast table. Ella didn't bother to reply. It wasn't worth it. She could see how things were and couldn't understand why she was feeling so disappointed. Why should she be? She wasn't usually like that.

'Ella was quite sober when I picked her up,' replied Loukas. Ella smiled at his defence of her. What would Anna have said if she'd known that he'd literally picked her up and carried her into the house?

'Why aren't you dressed, Costas?' asked Anna. The little boy made a face. 'It's time you were.'

'Ella was reading me a story.' Ella almost laughed. It was the worst thing Costas could have said. 'I liked it — very much. Why don't *you* read me stories, Anna?'

'Because I am always too busy cleaning up after you and your father,' snapped Anna.

'You're in a bad mood today,' added Loukas.

'I have things on my mind. Private things.'

'Sorry,' he said, winking at Ella. She knew he'd sensed the hostility between them, which made her feel rather silly and uncomfortable.

'I need to be getting back,' she said. 'The omelette was wonderful. Perhaps I shall see you again soon, Costas?'

'When? When will you come again?' asked the little boy. Ella bent down.

'I shall see you at school,' she said.

'I don't go to school.'

'You're not old enough?' said Ella, thinking she had made a mistake about his age.

'I am! I'm six and a half,' replied Costas indignantly.

'That's enough, Costas,' interrupted Loukas. 'I'm sure we shall be seeing

Ella again.'

'Certainly. If you want to.' At that moment, Anna coughed violently.

'Are you all right?' asked Loukas, going over to her.

'I told you I am not well.'

'I was wondering why you didn't see Ella at the festival?' He waited for an explanation from Anna, who only started washing up, so he added, 'You didn't go?' Anna nodded. 'We had family business to attend to. Neither was I well.'

'Anna's family has many vines to look after,' Loukas said, but Ella could see by his face that he wasn't particularly impressed.

Anna was glaring at her now. Ella could see that the other girl viewed her as a rival which was totally ridiculous, seeing as she was only acquainted with Loukas, which in this case had been inevitable. She wondered momentarily if she taught any of Anna's family and made a mental note to watch out. She didn't want to make any enemies in the village. Her work was too important and any kind of scandal could cost her job. 'Now I think I should be going. I'll just go upstairs and check I haven't left anything.' She retreated.

Up in the pretty bedroom, she looked round. Maybe the clothes in the wardrobe belonged to Anna? She wasn't going to think about that. After making sure she'd left nothing, she came down. Anna was standing with Loukas. 'Thank you so much,' Ella said. 'And thank you, Costas. I'm sure I shall see you at school soon.'

'I want to come with you and Daddy.'

'You're staying with Anna. Daddy has some things to see to in town.' Costas looked so sad that Ella bent and kissed him impulsively. Then she put her hand out to Anna. 'It was nice to meet you, Anna. And . . .' She stopped, realising she was wondering whether she would kiss Loukas good-bye when he dropped her off at June's. Anna ignored her friendly gesture, consolidating her rudeness.

'Ready now?' he asked. 'I shan't be very long. Maybe an hour.' Anna was glaring again.

'I may give my cold to Costas,' she said, going over to Loukas. 'Can't she take a taxi?' Ella was amazed at how rude she could be.

'No, she can't. She has been my

guest and her car is badly damaged. Be good for Anna, Costas.' His son didn't say anything but ran off in the direction of the garden. 'Come, Ella.' He turned and walked out.

She watched him swing himself up into the driver's seat of the big 4x4 and waited until he backed out on to the road. She could see her own little car in the distance and shuddered. A moment later he leaned over and opened the door for her.

'Are you all right?' He had changed from brusque to sympathetic.

'I was looking at the car.'

'I'll get someone to tow it down the mountain. Don't worry, I know him. It won't be that expensive.'

'Thank you. But I wasn't worried about that. It just — scared me a bit to look at it. I was thinking what if . . .'

' "What ifs" don't help,' he said. 'You're safe and that's all that matters. A car's only a lump of metal. And in my past profession I saw plenty of bodies that couldn't be mended.'

'Don't,' she said. A long silence ensued as he drove expertly down through the series of bends. 'I hope to see Costas at school in September. Has he been ill as I haven't seen him before.'

'No, he's very healthy.' No explanation followed, but she mentally made a note to make sure she looked Costas up on the school records. She changed the subject. 'I don't think Anna liked me,' she said.

'Don't worry about her. She was in

a bad mood. Probably because she didn't go to the festival. She can be a bit . . .' He seemed lost for words. 'But she's not usually quite as rude as that.'

'I don't mind. It must have been a shock to her seeing me there.'

'Why?' he asked and she was sure she had said the wrong thing. Maybe she was used to him bringing girls home for the night. But, somehow, she didn't think so. Ella felt she'd done enough prying into his private life, so she didn't ask any more questions. They confined themselves to chatting about the weather and other mundane things until the villa came into sight.

Loukas drew up outside the wrought-iron gates. 'Aren't you coming in?' she asked.

'No. As I told Costas, I shan't be long.' No, you told Anna that, she thought.

'Well then,' she said awkwardly, 'Thank you again and — *athio.*' She put out her hand to say a formal goodbye but he ignored it and jumped down from the driver's seat. She watched him come round and then open the passenger door. He put up his arms and she slid into them. 'It's very high,' she murmured to cover her confusion.

'Please don't say *athio,*' he said, looking down at her.

'What should I say?'

'*Ya sou.* I am your friend.' He smiled.

'*Ya sou* then, Loukas. And I am your friend too.' He paused and took a small card from his shirt pocket.

She stared at it. 'It's my phone number,' he said. 'Just in case you would like to get in touch again.'

'Thank you.' A second later, to Ella's surprise, he bent and kissed her on both cheeks. Her heart gave a little leap. She knew that Greeks reserved such intimacies for only family and very good friends. His kisses were still warm on her face. She touched her cheek as he walked back round the truck and drove off. She was breathless as she turned and hurried up the drive to the villa.

She was met at the door by June, who threw her arms about her. 'I have been *so* worried,' she said.

'But you knew where I was.'

'That's why,' replied June.

'What do you mean? You said you knew Loukas.'

'I do! In fact, everyone does!'

'But that's more worrying,' cried Ella.

'Don't let's stand here on the step. Come in and I'll make you a nice cup of coffee. You look like you need a perk.' Ella followed her friend, feeling extremely anxious. What could possibly be wrong with Loukas that everyone knew about?

CHAPTER 4

The awning outside the villa fluttered in a soft breeze. It was going to be another perfect day. The morning sun was warm as it struck Ella's back as she sat by the pool, its surface resembling the glassy blue-mint lollies she had loved as a child. That day she was wearing a pretty halter neck *pareo* over her bikini. At June's she could wear what she liked without pretence. Being with June was — comfortable!

'You look nice,' commented her friend, who was in the process of setting down a tray with two pretty cups

and matching milk and sugar jugs.
Ever since June had first come out to
Rhodes, she had kept up the ritual of
serving both coffee for elevenses and
tea at three. Being an ex-pat for years
hadn't made any difference. She
worked on English time and had suc-
ceeded in even converting her late
husband to the practice. 'Here you
are.' She handed over a cup to Ella,
who took it gratefully.

The burgeoning warmth of the sun
could have made Ella forget about
the events of the night before, but
was not succeeding. In fact, she
couldn't get Loukas out of her mind.
It was a long time since she'd been
interested in someone like this. Curiosity was clawing at her. One way or
another, she was going to find out the
truth and June was going to be the

one to tell her!

Her friend was sitting, legs crossed, sipping tea and contemplating the landscape. It was such a studied pose that Ella knew instinctively June realised what was coming. Her landlady was very good at allowing people to take their time over things. Now *was* the time. Ella put down her teacup. 'June, please will you tell me about Loukas?'

'Ah, Loukas. I thought that was coming. Made a hit, has he?' June laughed. Ella smiled. Her friend had probably seen the little by-play between them when they said goodbye. She didn't miss much.

'I don't know about a hit,' said Ella, 'but he is very interesting.'

'I'm sure lots of young women have said that about him. But he's a one-

woman man.' A throb of disappointment went through Ella, which she
discounted. Perhaps June meant
Anna. The girl's beautiful, but dis-
agreeable, face rose in her mind.

'Tell me more,' she said.

'Ah, his ideal woman . . .' June
sounded as if she was reluctant to
continue. Ella stared at her. She
couldn't bear not knowing as she
thought of all those lovely clothes and
the beautiful room she'd slept in.

'Is it Anna?' she said.

'Oh, you've met her then. No, not
Anna! She's a shifty piece of work.'

'What makes you say that?' asked
Ella, cheering up.

'I have my reasons. I'm not one to
gossip.'

'Of course not.' Ella continued to
sip her coffee, then said, 'Loukas said

she comes from a wine-producing family.'

'I shan't be drinking that vintage then,' joked Ella. 'Now, back to Loukas. The one-woman thing.'

'It has nothing to do with Anna,' replied June. 'I'm referring to Loukas' wife.'

'His wife?' Ella felt a throb of disappointment.

'I mean his *late* wife.'

'Oh.' Ella drank the rest of her coffee and replaced the cup carefully. Loukas' wife was dead! How awful! 'How did she . . . die?'

'It was a tragic accident. A crash on the mountain.' Ella must have looked horrified, because June said, 'I know it's a shock, but that's how we all felt when it happened.'

'Was it long ago?'

'Well . . .' June calculated. 'Three, maybe four years?'

'Oh, no! That meant Costas was only a toddler.'

'Yes. Loukas has brought him up by himself. He dotes on the boy.'

'Well, he's a lovely little chap,' said Ella, thinking of that enchanting smile. 'Tell me about . . . ?' she fished.

'Xanthe,' explained June. 'Xanthe and Loukas were soul mates. Strangely enough, she was a teacher too, but not primary. Although she used to teach at the village school for a while, she found a much more suitable job on another island where the big College is. She used to leave Costas with Loukas who only works part-time. They needed the money, I suppose.' June looked uncertain at that point.

Ella thought of him carrying her so easily in a fire-fighter's hold. 'Please tell me more about the accident?' She was thinking of her own.

'She was driving down the mountain, when the car overturned on the bend. There was a local man involved in the crash, but he left the scene. The car ended upside down in a deep hollow. Then it burst into flames. She couldn't get out.' Ella was horror-struck.

'What an awful way to die!'

'That was why I was concerned when you decided to come home so late. You never know who's on the road, nor what state they're in.' Ella shuddered at the thought. 'In Xanthe's case, I don't exactly know the circumstances, but what they were was never proved. And her passenger was influential.' June sighed. 'Unfortunately, it was Loukas who found his wife. I won't go into details. But . . .' she paused, 'I heard it was difficult to identify her. Nobody should die like that. Loukas arrived quickly because the Fire Service was called out and, naturally he got there first, but he couldn't do a thing.'

'How terrible!' cried Ella. 'But who was looking after Costas then?'

'Probably Anna. She'd been working for them for some time and baby-sat regularly as well as looking after the house. Loukas never recovered. He doesn't work very much now, except for doing some forestry. That is, unless he's needed desperately.'

'I can imagine,' cried Ella, feeling so sorry for him. No wonder he was upset when he found her trapped in her car.

'I think he isn't up to it any more. It's such a tough job. I believe he helps out with the forest fires sometimes, when it's so hot and the trees are like dry sticks. Over here, they take volunteers as well as career firemen. I expect he's still an asset to them having trained for it.'

'I remember how my father wouldn't bring us over here sometimes because of the fires. But how does Loukas manage now without a job. It's a lovely house.'

'Well . . .' June leaned forward. 'I've heard that Xanthe had a big life insurance. At least that's what people say, but who'd want money from tragedy.'

I bet Takis would, thought Ella.

'We all thought Loukas might move

from the house,' added June, 'but he stayed on and although I've never been there, people who have say that he's kept her room untouched. Like a shrine. I would have thought he'd have got rid of all the stuff by now. Maybe found himself someone else. It's a lonely place up there.'

'Yes,' replied Ella quietly. June stared at her. 'I slept in that room, you know.'

'Good heavens,' said June. 'He must have been taken with you.'

'There wasn't anywhere else,' replied Ella, 'and he wouldn't let me go home.'

'What was it like?' asked June. Ella regarded her.

'Beautiful. She must have been a woman of taste.'

'Clothes?'

'Wardrobes full. Also books and lovely furniture.'

'Did you get a look at the clothes?' June seemed genuinely interested.

'Only peeked. A lot of them were designer. She must have been a social butterfly. Not at all like a teacher, although I suppose she had to go to functions.' She leaned back and was glad that June couldn't see her eyes behind her sunglasses. Now it was all making sense. That was why Loukas had been angry with her. Why he'd called her stupid for driving down the mountain at night. The tortured look on his face in the lounge, must have brought Xanthe's crash back. And when Ella had crashed, it must have been terrible. Poor Loukas — and poor Xanthe. Ella stared at the sea, which seemed to have gone darker.

'He must have liked you,' repeated June, bringing her back to reality.

'I don't think he had any option,' replied Ella. 'What about Anna?'

'Oh, well, *she* has her hooks in him now,' said June.

'I could see that, but he didn't seem very keen.'

'I told you, he's a one-woman man — and he certainly wouldn't want Anna.'

'Well, why is she working for him?' asked Ella. 'Why doesn't he give her the sack?'

'There are reasons, which sooner or later, you'll find out the way you're going!'

'What do you mean?' June ignored her question and changed the subject. So there was still some mystery about Loukas.

'What's important is you seem to be the first woman he's been taken with for a very long time. That is, from what I saw from the upstairs window.'

'You are naughty, June! You were watching us,' accused Ella. 'And we didn't do anything.'

'But you seemed to be very good friends!' Suddenly, the darkness of Ella's earlier mood lifted and the sun was shining again. 'I'm glad I've cheered you up,' added June and gave Ella a knowing look. 'More coffee? I'm going to have another cup.' They sat, both lost in their own thoughts.

'June?'

'Yes?'

'Have you any idea if Costas goes to school? He's not on the register.'

'I think he's home-educated,' replied June. 'People say that Loukas is scared to let him out of his sight. It's a pity because a child needs to go to school and meet other children. Is home schooling illegal?'

'I don't know here. I'd have to look it up, but I agree with what you said about mixing with other children.' Ella was thinking. Costas didn't seem as though home education was doing him any harm, in fact, the reverse. He was very bright and articulate. But June was right. It must be quite lonely for the little boy in that isolated house on the mountain. She supposed that Costas was left with Anna, whenever Loukas went out somewhere he couldn't take his son, which couldn't be a particularly good solution. She, herself, had seen Anna snap at him. But maybe she was in

just a bad temper as Loukas said.
Maybe she was cheerful most times.
But who did Costas *play* with?

Ella's brain was computing the
advantages and the drawbacks. The
latter won, because it was nothing to
do with her really. But then she
decided it was, because she was the
school teacher. Maybe someone —
her for instance, should go and see
Loukas and talk to him. But, then,
again, she hardly knew him. However, he had said they were friends.
Her cheeks felt quite hot when she
thought of his kiss. She told herself
off for being so silly. She was not a
teenager. She'd had several boy-
friends and they hadn't been backwards coming forwards. She was a
sophisticated girl, well-travelled and
certainly used to handling men. Look

at the way she had been able to put off Takis. And he was a Greek!

Loukas didn't seem Greek somehow. He was measured, not volatile, and almost taciturn. But he had a temper too.

'Penny for them,' said June.

'Oh, sorry, I was only thinking that I might . . .'

'Find out about Costas?'

'How did you know?'

'I just did,' smiled June, 'but remember what I said. Loukas isn't an easy man to cope with.'

'June, I was thinking about Costas!'

'I know you were, love, but these days anything can happen.' Her eyes sparkled. 'I'm an uncontrollable matchmaker.'

'Well, don't try it on me, please. At present, I have too much to do to bother with men,' said Ella.

'Point taken. Now what have you planned for what's left of this beautiful day?' asked June. 'I'd suggest a rest after the events of last night.'

'I'm perfectly all right,' returned Ella. 'In fact, I have quite a lot of preparation to do for September. I have to start sometime." She stood up. 'And — I need to tidy up my room!'

'How boring,' teased June. 'I have a suggestion. When you've finished as much as you can take, we can go down to the *taverna* for dinner. I miss going out since I lost Dimitri. That's of course if you want to be seen with an old woman like me!'

'You say that every time, and you're not old,' exclaimed Ella. 'In fact, I have to work hard to keep up with you. It's a deal.' She held out her hand in fun.

'Done!' said June. 'Let's make it about eight?'

'Agreed.'

'And you never know, you might find out a bit more about Loukas.'

'You're wicked,' laughed Ella.

'I know.' A moment later, the two of them were clearing the patio table.

Ella had been to June's favourite *taverna* in Rhodes Town several times. It was some distance but it was worth it for the service and the food. Of course, everyone knew June, which was a bonus. She and Dimitri had been very popular and, according to her friend had cut quite a dash on the small, intimate dance floor. They were lucky enough to park in the road outside and strolled in through the arch which led into a a series of small cobbled back streets — or rather lanes. Ella loved the sound of the birds, twittering away in their pretty cages, although she was sorry for them because they should have been free. But that was the Greek way. The song birds were ornaments, just like the wind chimes, mainly constructed of a variety of bells that tinkled in the warm wind which was so different from the wind that blew off the mountain. Here, everything was snug and pretty, rather than wild and beautiful.

This was the tourists' Rhodes and plenty were strolling through the arches and mooching about in the shops looking for bargains. Probably many of them came from the variety of yachts and the sleek, white ocean liner that dwarfed all the other ships in the harbour. But a very good table had been reserved for June and Ella.

'It's so lovely,' said Ella, looking round. 'So peaceful.'

'It is now,' replied the practical June, 'but as you know when the clubs and cafés empty in the early hours of the morning, most of the clientèle won't even know the way home. And, unfortunately, a great many of them are English.'

'Well, it's good for the taxi trade,' joked Ella, but she knew how June felt. Embarrassed, although she should have been used to it by now. 'At least we'll be home before then.'

'We certainly will! Hi, Athina . . .' she greeted the waitress. 'I'm having my favourite tonight.'

'Lamb with okra?' smiled Ella.

'What else?' replied June. 'How about you?'

'I'm not sure,' she replied looking at the menu. Very soon, she said, 'I'm going to try the beef. I love the baby onions and herbs with it. Beef *stifado*, please, Athina, with *horiatiki*.'

'You're turning into a real Greek!' complimented June.

'No wonder with this kind of food.'

Their food was accompanied by a very lively accordion player, until June laughingly waved him off. 'Go away, Alex.' He grinned and moved on to the next table. They chatted and things were livening up around them, when a hand touched Ella's shoulder. She jumped.

'Takis!' she said, catching sight of June's face, which clearly said, Get rid of him. He was wearing an open-necked shirt and jeans and smiling in the most charming manner.

'Ella, what a surprise!' He looked sincere, but Ella had a feeling that maybe he had seen the car and come looking for her. 'And June.' He gave a tiny bow and she nodded to him curtly. 'May I buy you both a drink?'

'Oh, I'm driving.' Ella didn't want him to buy a drink for her. He needed only a little encouragement and she'd never get rid of him.

'We have a bottle already,' gestured June.

'Then you must have another. The best.' Ella could see he wasn't taking no for an answer. He turned and beckoned Athina. 'My usual, please.' He stood there and there was nothing they could do, but invite him to sit down! 'Ella, I was *desolate* to hear you have been in an accident.' He looked so sincere, she almost believed him. But, although his charm might have worked on other girls, it didn't with Ella.

'How did you know about my accident?' asked Ella.

'From Anna, my cousin. You have met her.'

'Yes.' So Anna was his cousin and probably a spy. It didn't take her long to tell everyone about me, thought Ella, remembering Anna's scowl. I hope she didn't inform everybody I was sleeping with him!

'As I told you, it was inadvisable to drive off after the fiesta!' His *I told you so* attitude made Ella angry. Who did he think he was telling her what to do? If, perhaps, he hadn't been so

pushy then she might have taken u
his offer to stay in the village but
now, she was glad she didn't, even
though her car had been wrecked.
But a moment later, her sensible side
took over. If she had taken Takis'
advice, she might not have risked her
life. On the other hand, she would
probably have risked losing her job
because after a night under Takis'
parents' roof she was sure she'd tell
him what she really thought of him.

'Are you enjoying yourself?' asked
Takis. Then he turned to June. 'I assume you have shown Ella all our
sights here in Rhodes?'

'All she wants to see,' replied June.
Ella could see that she was forcing
herself to be civil to Takis.

'Is that so, Ella? Then you will not
be interested in taking your pupils to

one of the wonderful archaeological ruins that is not too far from our village? They are never too young to hear about our culture. The trip has been introduced to them and they can't wait to go, which is next Wednesday by the way.'

Ella felt very cross with him, arranging things without letting her know. 'Which site?' asked Ella, knowing she was on difficult ground. She was the teacher; he was a governor and she did not want to look unwilling.

'It is reputed to be the site of the palace and the promontory where King Aegeus saw the black sail hoisted.'

'You mean the myth of when Theseus forgot to change the colour of the sail and his father threw himself from the cliff top, thinking his son

was dead?'

'Very good.' Takis nodded.

'But rather inappropriate for such young children,' replied Ella. 'Anyway, I didn't think that was Rhodes, but Athens,' replied Ella glibly. June gave her the thumbs up when Takis wasn't looking.

'The old legends are very good for tourists,' grinned Takis.

'However, I would not like to give the children the wrong information,' said Ella. She could see that he knew she was not fooled. 'But I'd be delighted to take them.'

'Good, because I have arranged it. I shall be coming along of course.'

'You arranged it without asking me?' Ella felt annoyed.

'I knew you would agree. Next week then. I'm really looking forward to it.

As are some of the parents, who will come along to help. We need chaperones.' He smiled at his own joke.

'Humph!' June sniffed, while Ella ignored the inference.

'Now, would you like to dance?' Takis was looking across at the small dance floor, where two couples were already embracing.

'I'm not feeling like it,' replied Ella.

'Nevertheless, it would be a pity to waste such a wonderful evening.' His dark eyes glittered in the candlelight and a moment later, he was pulling her to her feet.

'Really, Takis, I'm sorry, but . . .'

'I too shall be sorry if you refuse.'

'Very well, but only one. I told you I'm tired.'

'After last night?' he whispered as

he took her in his arms. She withdrew as much as she could.

'The accident shook me up.'

'Ah, yes, the accident.' He was holding her close. It would have looked bad to struggle. Instead, she breathed in, deciding whatever happened she was not going to give him any encouragement whatsoever. She was already smarting at the remark. Evidently Anna had indicated Ella had slept with Loukas. As they moved slowly, she caught June's look. It was a half-grimace.

'And . . . what did you think of Mr. Loukas Milas?'

'I don't really see what that has got to do with you, Takis.'

'Indeed it has. In fact, Mr. Milas is in a very dangerous position, although of course he must find the situation difficult.'

'What do you mean?' Ella brought their clinch to a halt. 'What has he done?'

'In short, I am almost sure he is breaking the law.'

'How?'

'Let us continue our dance. I was enjoying it — and I think you were too.'

'I told you I'm tired. I'm not in the mood for dancing. Please go on with what you were saying.'

'I can explain later.' He flashed her an insincere smile.

'Later?'

'I was hoping to take you on to see some more of our wonderful town.'

'I don't think so,' replied Ella. 'You may remember that I was brought up here? Rhodes Town is well-known to me. Now, what were you saying about Loukas? What has he done that is illegal?'

'He has been keeping his child out of school. At present, I am looking into it. I hardly know how to say this, but your association with Loukas Milas may also compromise you.' He was looking down at her with a half-smile.

'Are you threatening me?' Ella asked.

'No, only pointing out the fact that the man is being investigated.'

'You realise that he appears to have no option given his personal circumstances!' broke out Ella.

'Ah, he has told you about his unfortunate personal position?'

'He told me nothing,' remonstrated Ella.

'Perhaps someone else has mentioned it to you?'

'Who could have?'

'June, of course.' Her friend was watching them closely. 'June is in the position of telling you whatever she likes. Mine is the official position.'

'I think we should finish this conversation now, please,' said Ella, turning away and making for her table.

'Certainly,' replied Takis, following her. 'Please remember that I have told you this for your own good.'

'I'm sure,' replied Ella, sitting down.

'Is anything the matter?' asked June.

'Ella is very tired and in the circumstances I think it would be better if I left,' replied Takis. He waved to the waitress as Ella sat there silently. 'I shall be paying for anything these ladies have had,' he said. 'Thank you,

Ella — and June, for allowing me to share your table. I shall see you soon, Ella, and I am sure that the children will find the trip most educational. I look forward to it.'

Ella only nodded. He gave a little bow and they watched him walk away.

'What the hell was he up to?' asked June in her forthright way.

'He wanted to find out if I knew anything about Loukas,' said Ella. 'The man's insufferable.'

'Did you say I told you?'

'Of course not!'

'Thank goodness for that — and for how you feel about him,' replied June. 'By the way he was holding you, I was afraid you were enjoying it.'

'Don't, June, I can't bear it.'

'Good, well, after that, let's get on

with the evening and forget about Takis,' said June. 'Then, later, you can tell me *exactly* what he said. I'm all ears.' June leaned forward, her large earrings jangling.

CHAPTER 5

'I've looked it up in teaching regulations,' said Ella, 'and, unfortunately, whatever we think of Takis, I'm afraid he's right about Costas. He should be in school and, if he isn't, then Loukas is in trouble.'

'I don't think he'll be worried about that,' replied June, 'given his present state of mind and, anyway, Takis may have had a good reason to make you suspicious.'

'Don't you mean threaten?' cried Ella. 'What other reason could he have?'

'Ella, can't you see he's jealous?' June said quickly. 'For such an intelligent girl, you can be very naïve.'

'Jealous of Loukas and me? There is nothing between us. Good heavens. I've only just met the man,' countered Ella. 'I'm not in the market for one-night stands!'

'Don't be offended, dear, but anyone could tell he made an impression. In fact, I'd bet my gossipy life on it that he's been on your mind ever since he kissed your cheek.' Ella's eyes said it all.

'I suppose he did — in a way. After all, he did come to help — and I couldn't have done without him.'

'Doubtless that's what Anna told her cousin. There's nothing to choose between the two of them. Not a particularly nice family, I'm afraid.

Or maybe that's too harsh. Takis' mother is perfectly polite, but his father — well . . .' June rolled her eyes. 'If Dimitri was here, he'd tell you about Takis' dad. Like father, like son, I say.'

'Are you going to tell me then?'

'Let's save that for another time. So, what are you going to do to help Costas, considering how much you'd like to help them both.' Her eyes twinkled.

'Don't be so naughty, June. I really do have Costas' interests at heart, even though his dad is so good with him. Maybe I'll start with the trip.'

'You mean to the archaeological ruins? Don't let Takis bully you into going,' June looked slightly worried. 'Although I suppose . . .' she sighed, 'he's . . .'

'He's one of my bosses.'

'And you think it would be advisable?'

'Well, it's a way of getting Costas to come. I'm sure he would love to be with the other children.' replied Ella. 'I'm really sorry for him, isolated in that house on the mountain.'

'You really think Loukas will agree?'

'I shall have to try and persuade him,' said Ella, at the same time wondering how exactly she was going to manage it. 'Now, I ought to go and swot up about this place I'm supposed to be going. I can't look an idiot.'

'You'll never be that. I assume you've been there before?'

'I think so,' replied Ella uncertainly.

'I can't see the children enjoying it,'

110

replied June doubtfully. 'It's only a heap of old ruins.' Ella began to laugh.

'You've been in Rhodes for years. I'm sure Dimitri wouldn't have approved you calling Greek civilisation "a heap of old ruins".'

'He had a great sense of humour. I miss him.'

'I'm sure you do.' Ella put her hand on to June's arm. 'Now, I suppose I should ring Loukas and broach the idea.'

'You do that,' replied June.

'Wish me luck!' As she thought of how he'd kissed her, Ella was already wondering if asking for her to spend a whole day with Costas was a good idea.

Ella's heart was beating very fast

when she phoned. 'Loukas?' she said. Thank goodness he was in.

'Ella?' She loved the way he pronounced her name!

'Yes.'

'You are phoning about the car? I am afraid it is not ready yet. In fact, my friend has not even been to collect it. But I am very pleased to hear from you.'

'Good . . .' She thought this might be one of the most awkward calls she had ever made. Then she pulled herself together, at the same time asking herself why she should think so. She was being stupid. 'No, I'm not ringing about the car.' There was silence, then he replied,

'You're not?'

'No.' She went straight to the point. 'It's about Costas.'

'What about him?' Loukas' voice was level. She thought for a moment that he must be offended. 'He is very well and, by the way, he has been asking about you. You seem to have made a great impression.'

'Gosh.' Another silence.

'I'm glad you didn't throw away my card.' The words were unexpected.

'I wouldn't do that. Besides, I would like to see you again!' The invitation came out so easily and then she told herself off for sounding so eager.

'About Costas?'

'That's right. But I don't have a car.'

'I could come and pick you up,' he offered. That was what she wanted to hear. 'Maybe we could have dinner?'

'That would be lovely. I really wanted to talk to you very soon. You see the school, well, I am taking them on a trip and . . . But that's what I wanted to see you about . . .' She trailed off.

'I could make it tonight as long as Anna will babysit.'

'That would be great.' She imagined Anna's face if he told her where he was going. But, Ella thought, he won't do that or she won't be very accommodating but, if she wouldn't, he could bring Costas along, which wouldn't be ideal. 'What time?'

'Eightish?'

'Fine. I'll be ready. Thank you.' She couldn't think of anything else to say.

'*Athio,* Ella.' He sounded so formal, but then he added, 'No, *Ya sou.*' She could hear the smile in his voice.

'*Ya sou,* Loukas.' She was remembering how his kiss felt on her cheek as she put the handset down.

The remainder of the day passed very slowly in spite of Ella swotting up on the ancient site where they were going on the trip. A lot of the history she knew already; that in ancient times Cretans came over from their island and lived on Rhodes, which gave some credence to the legend of the old king who threw himself on to the rocks crazed with grief because he thought his son had been killed by the Minotaur, who roamed the Cretan labyrinth. It was a tragic story. If she had been feeling cynical she would have put it down to the fact it was excellent tourist material, but the old tale was also very romantic. Theseus was so in love with Ariadne, who had led him to safety with a ball of thread that he forgot everything else and didn't change the sail to white.

A thought flew into Ella's head like a butterfly. Had she the power to make Loukas forget his sadness at the death of his wife? Then she squashed it. What are you doing, Ella, she asked herself, imagining such a thing? Remember you weren't going to get involved in any relationship. Every one she'd experienced so far had ended in tears. She put down her Biro, dragging herself back to reality. She'd satisfied Takis professionally and that was all he was going to get; to tell the children.

By the time six o' clock arrived, Ella had tried on almost everything she had in her wardrobe, except swim-wear. June had looked in on her to check she didn't want any supper. The expression on her face said it all.

'You don't know what to wear for Loukas.'

'I just want to look nice. I'm not doing it especially for him.'

After showering, putting on her prettiest skin tone underwear, and after doing her hair, Ella slipped into the dress she'd chosen. The muted tones of the silk-chiffon showed off her tan. A satisfied feeling warmed her. Perfect. Then she chose her favourite light wrap. Her shoes had been another extravagance. High-heeled in the same shade. A clutch bag was the finishing touch, but what should she wear round her neck? She chose a delicate golden butterfly necklace and on her wrist a matching bracelet.

At quarter to eight, she decided to go down, suddenly feeling shy at what might be June's reaction. It was 'Wow!'

'Thank you,' she said. 'I thought it was all right.'

'More than all right,' said the older woman. 'It's stunning!' She looked through the window into the flower-scented evening as they heard a car approaching.

'You know, Ella, you might have brought that man alive. He's been dead too,' said June. Ella could see the car's headlights at the bottom of the drive. Then they switched off. Should she wait for him to come to fetch her?

She didn't have to wait long. Then June was at the door. 'Hello, Loukas. Yes, she's ready. I'll just call her.'

Seconds later, Ella was looking into his dark eyes.

'You look . . . wonderful.' She thrilled at the compliment.

'Thank you,' she said. 'And you look pretty good too.' They smiled at each other as with a wave to June, they walked off down the drive.

'I hope you don't hold last night against me?'

'Of course not.'

'I've been told I'm morose.'

'By whom?' asked Ella, as he was holding the door open for her. He didn't answer.

'It doesn't matter. Oh, I have cleaned out the truck. You will not get your dress dirty.' She was touched. She got in, very conscious of his eyes on her legs, then arranged her dress as he went round to the driver's side. As he started up she noticed how brown and strong his hands were. It was true. He looked very good. He wasn't wearing a tie, but an impressive summer suit, which was a shimmering light grey and tailored to make the most of his broad shoulders and narrow hips. She was glad that she had dressed-up as he wouldn't have looked out of place in any smart restaurant.

'Have you travelled much, Loukas?' she asked.

'Some. Why do you want to know?'

'Well, I was just wondering if you were born on the island?'

'No, but my father was.'

'And?'

'Is this twenty questions? If so, I'm willing to answer about three!' he smiled. 'I promise you, they're not that interesting. My father was Greek. He was a farmer. I left for the main-land when I was sixteen and saw a fair bit of Europe. Then I came back. That wasn't particularly inspiring, was it?'

'I'm sorry. I'm always interested in people's backgrounds.' Ella decided that she would tell him a bit about her family, even though he wasn't prepared to say much about his. 'Years ago, I lived in Rhodes.'

'So, what did your father do?'

'He was in the Diplomatic Service.' That was as much as Ella was going to say.

'Well! A diplomat's daughter. That's why you speak Greek so well.'

'My father's always been in love with Greece. He used to tell me the most fascinating stories. That's why I like visiting archaeological sites so much.' She was getting near to broaching the subject which was high on her agenda.

'Oh, yes,' he said dryly, 'we Greeks are very proud of our myths and don't mind bending them a little. But I suppose it's your vocation as a teacher to straighten them out.'

'No, to fit the fiction around the facts. All children love stories.'

'You're very impressive. No wonder you got the job.' They drove on and Ella realised they were going up into the mountains again. He must have caught her looking and added, 'Don't worry, I know what I'm doing.'

'Why should I be worried?' she replied.

'No reason,' he said, 'but I thought you might think we were going to run into a deer. There's plenty of *dama* roaming round in this forest.' The corners of his mouth curved into a smile as he handled another hairpin faster than she'd ever dare. If she hadn't known his temperament she would have thought he was being deliberately annoying. But she was determined to enjoy herself. He's just being a man, she thought. And a very good-looking one. However, on the other hand, she realised inside he was hiding a deep sadness, which made him seem almost vulnerable, in spite of his flashes of wit.

'That's where we're going,' he said. 'Down there.' Ella could see a glimpse of white through the trees. 'My favourite haunt.' For a second, she wondered if he used to bring Xanthe. Of course, he did, if it was his special place.

'Is it a hotel?' she asked as they swung off the road and down a steep track.

'It's a hunting lodge.'

'Oh.' Ella disliked hunting.

'It's all right, Ella, I hardly ever use my gun these days.' His perception was surprising. 'And I'm sure you'll like it.'

'I'm certain of that,' she said.

The drive now led into a curved space from which another drive led out. A few vehicles, much like his, were parked neatly.

'It's quite popular,' he said, 'but I've booked.'

The lodge was spectacular from the outside. In fact it looked like it had been spirited from the Swiss Alps and been planted there. It was very large having three floors and the outside was painted white with a wide ornamented arch for a main door. The windows were arched too with small leaded panes and below them, black criss-cross beans contrasted with the white walls making them stand out. Above them all along the second floor was a long wooden balcony, while another floor at the top had more balconies and three-sided arches. In fact, it was quite beautiful.

'It's wonderful,' she said, 'but it doesn't look Greek.'

'It's actually Italian and was built in the 1920s. It's managed to keep its original character even when it was refurbished a couple of years ago. On the other side the view's magnificent.'

'I can't wait,' she said, smiling back.

They entered the oak-beamed hall and Ella tried not to look at the hunting trophies on the walls, which were a bizarre mixture of deer and boar heads. They walked through to a delightful restaurant, which was, as Loukas had said, decorated in the Twenties style, with great palms in pots and a long window running across the breadth of the wall. 'Let's have a drink first,' he said, 'well, at least, you can. I'm driving.'

'I don't drink very much,' she said, thinking of the fiery traditional liqueur that the Greeks liked as an aperitif. 'I'll have a spritzer.' She could see that their entrance had been noticed by the other diners, who looked mainly Greek. Then the *maitre d'* appeared and led them forward. The man's dark eyes were appraising but inquisitive. Seconds later, he was leading them to their table. He held out her chair as she sat down in the small candle-lit alcove that Loukas had chosen. As Ella sat down, she gasped as she saw the view.

'It's wonderful,' she said. The whole of the landscape was a mixture of sultry red light from the setting sun and pure darkness, only broken up into twinkling masses which must have been towns and villages.

'I'm glad you like it. His eyes swivelled from the landscape and met hers. Again sadness and pleasure were mixed. Was he thinking about Xanthe? 'You do look lovely,' he said.

'Thank you.' For some reason the simple compliment was one of the nicest she'd ever been paid. They picked up their drinks. The spritzer almost cooled the heat she felt inside and out. He was drinking some kind of bottled juice.

'Hungry?' he asked and she nodded in reply. A moment later, he was looking across to the bar and immediately the *maitre d'* appeared once more and said, 'The waiter will be over to take your order, sir. Here are the menus.'

'Thank you,' Loukas nodded. Watching him, she thought briefly that perhaps this was where Xanthe sat opposite her husband. They must have been deeply in love. As he studied his menu, she knew why. What woman wouldn't be in love with him? It was so sad that he had lost Xanthe, but — she came back to herself — if he hadn't, then she wouldn't have been here. She knew she was being selfish. Then she looked down at the extensive menu and was glad she read Greek!

'What would you like?' he asked. 'An appetizer?'

'*Tsatsiki*, please.' She loved its delicate fragrance — Greek yoghurt with grated cucumber, accompanied by hot pitta bread.

'*Dalmadakia* for me.' She wasn't surprised. It was a man's choice. Fresh mincemeat and savoury rice, wrapped in vine leaves.

The starters were delicious and she treated herself to a glass of wine, which was the best she'd tasted for a long time — and said so.

'I'm glad you like it here,' he said, staring at her over the rim of his glass. 'Are you ready for the main course now?'

'Goodness,' she said, 'I'm almost full already.'

'I'm pleased you said, "almost"!' he joked. While they were waiting for it to be served, they indulged in small talk and Ella found herself telling him more and more about her own history as he skilfully avoided his. 'I'm really enjoying the evening,' he said and reaching out he laid his warm hand over hers, where she let it lie. His touch made her tingle and she felt a throb within her.

'I am too,' she replied. 'Thank you for asking me.'

'My pleasure. I haven't had such a good time for ages.' He took his hand away and she felt bereft. Her *Souvia Shaslic* arrived, succulent lamb, charcoal grilled and marvellously seasoned.

'My *Afella's* good,' he said, looking up. 'These fillets of pork are excellent!'

'My lamb too. Delicious.' A companionable silence ensued. It was a magical time. With the rapport between them and the wondrous view spread out before them.

'Loukas, I want to ask you something.'

'Fire away.' He folded his napkin and put it aside. 'Or would you like pudding first.'

'I couldn't possibly,' she said.

'Then neither could I.'

'Oh, please, don't let me put you off.'

'Well . . . okay.' She laughed at his expression, but again she knew he was steering her away from saying anything serious. She frowned.

His Baklava came, tiny sweet pastries with walnuts and almonds and drizzled all over with honey. A second later, he had speared one with his fork and offered it to her. She shook her head.

'Please,' he said, 'just one.' He was as irresistible as the pastry! As her mouth filled with honeyed sweetness, she was determined to say what she had come to say.

'Loukas . . .' He stopped eating.

'Yes.'

'I want to talk about . . .' she was going to add, 'Costas . . .' but thought better of it and said. '. . . About a trip I'm going on.'

'Oh,' he said and she could see the relief on his face and she was annoyed with herself. 'Where?'

'To an archaeological site. King Aegeus' palace. Next Wednesday. I'm sure you know it. I'm going to take some of my pupils with me.'

'You're brave,' he said. 'If they're anything like Costas, they'd rather go to the beach.'

'That's unhelpful,' she said.

'Sorry.' He looked sincere.

'It's always best to tell the truth.'

'I agree entirely,' he said.

'I want to tell the story to the children about the site first and then we shall go and look at it.' Then she plunged in. 'I would like to take Costas.' Silence. They regarded each other.

'Costas,' he repeated.

'Yes, I'm sure he would enjoy it.'

'Maybe. But he's not going.' She hadn't expected a flat refusal.

'Why ever not? I'm sure he'd enjoy it.'

'I expect he would, but he doesn't know the children.' She sensed hope and a reason to argue her case.

'He'd soon get to know them. Children are like that.' He smiled.

'You're a teacher. I'm a father. I know what Costas is like.'

'What is he like?' asked Ella, determined not to make this a proper argument. He shrugged.

'I know him.'

'*You* could come!' she said, not having meant to. He stared at her. 'There will be other parents.'

He was silent. He was going to *have* to give a reason why the two of them couldn't go. 'Maybe they won't want me along.'

'What gives you that idea?'

'I'm pretty sure.' He was staring at his glass. She could feel his discomfort.

'You know me,' she said, 'and I've asked you. I'm in charge.' She thought of how Takis would take it, but she didn't care.

'I'll think about it,' he said. 'When is this trip?' Her heart lifted.

'In a couple of days' time. I'll let you know the details.'

'I'm not promising.'

'Of course not.' Her reply was light.

'More Baklava?' he asked. His mood had changed and his eyes sparkled.

'No, you have it,' she said, 'I couldn't eat another mouthful.' He smiled. His moods shifted so fast that a sudden thought came to her. What would he be like to live with if they ever got together? Could she stand it? At that moment she didn't know the answer. All she was sure of was that Loukas was the most fascinating man she had ever met.

They made the evening last, staying for coffee, lingering on in the lovely lounge, staring at the stars hanging so low over the landscape that it seemed they could be caught in a fishing net.

'What are you thinking?' he asked. His voice was gentle.

'About my father.' Loukas' eyebrows lifted. 'The stars,' she added. 'He taught me how to identify them. "There's Orion with his bow," he'd say. "Look for the Plough. Its last star points North.".

'Yes, I was told about the gods and goddesses in the sky too.' He looked into her eyes. 'Cassiopeia and her golden chair. Castor and Pollux, the heavenly twins. Those old Greeks knew a thing or two. You see, Ella, we're quite alike.'

'Are we?' He nodded.

She looked into his eyes and wondered if he was feeling the same as she was; that she wanted this evening to last for ever. But the time to part had to come. Neither she nor Loukas were looking for a one-night stand. Even if they were, there would be no opportunity and, somehow, she felt, deep inside that such early intimacy would be a very big mistake. June said he was still in love with Xanthe. Ella didn't want to be a substitute for his dead wife. Not ever.

They sat in the car, having been

mostly silent all the way home. She knew he, like her, was wondering what to do. Her heart kept giving funny little jumps. Once they had reached the open road, after swinging down from the mountain, he had twice leaned towards her and taken her hand, but only for a moment, as if to assure her he cared. Perhaps he behaved like that to other girls he took out? He *must* have had other girlfriends since Xanthe, however briefly.

Ella told herself that if he never asked her out again, at least she'd got somewhere with Costas. Perhaps he would bring him on the trip? If so, it would be a breakthrough. One up on Takis, at least. But she wasn't going to even think about him and his fluid charm. She felt Takis had nothing honest about him. So unlike Loukas.

He brought the 4×4 to a stop outside June's. They didn't speak. The silence was almost unbearable and the atmosphere so thick with unspoken words that Ella could almost taste it. Outside the night was cool, but the heat between them was overpowering.

'We're here then,' he said. The anticlimax was almost a relief.

'Yes.' It was all she trusted herself to say.

'A great night.' He was staring through the windscreen.

'Yes.'

'I . . .' He turned to her. '. . . I want to do this again.'

'So do I.'

'Ella . . . I'm sorry.' Her heart lurched. Then this was goodbye. "I'm sorry I'm not good with words.' She could breathe again. She put out her hand and instinctively rested it on his thigh. If he had been anyone else, she wouldn't have made such a provocative gesture. He put his hand over hers and clasped it. She could feel the heat rising off him.

'I always say too much when I'm nervous,' she offered.

'Nervous — of me?' She had never seen amazement in his face before.

'Perhaps?' He laughed.

'I have to confess. I feel the same with you.'

'Why?' She stared at him.

'Because . . .' he shrugged. '. . . because you're . . . No,' he shook his head. 'I'm not making sense. I only wanted us to have a good night. To enjoy ourselves.'

'We did, and now . . .'

'We're here.' She nodded. It was a strange conversation. The kind you have when you're sixteen years old and shy, but the two of them were experienced adults. She'd had lovers, however briefly; he'd had a wife. What was the matter with them?

He leaned towards her and there was only a tiny space between them. When the kiss came, it was sweet and lingering, but as they both sensed that sweetness, it became more passionate. Her eyes were closed as his mouth sought hers, then she felt him draw back. It was agonising. Everything within her was streaming towards him, wanted to be with him. It was like severing two halves as he withdrew his arms but he was holding one of her hands tightly almost hurting her. Then his grip relaxed. She let her hand lie in his for a moment, then she withdrew it gently.

They were apart now, both breathing heavily. She looked up into his eyes, which seemed to burn as they probed her face. Then he turned as if he couldn't bear it any more and she knew he felt like she did. Cheated.

'No,' he said, in a voice almost too low to be heard, 'it's not fair.' He was staring out of the window as if she didn't exist.

'What, Loukas?'

'I can't explain.' He turned to her. 'Not now. But I hope I can. One day.' His breathing was still short and she realised that once more he was trying to control himself. If only he knew how very much she hadn't wanted him to stop. She looked away, her face flaring, glad that it was dark.

'I don't understand, Loukas.'

'I know,' he said gently. Then turning, he lifted his hand and brushed back a stray lock of her damp hair. The gesture wrenched her inside. 'But we will see each other again.'

'I hope so.'

'Don't be hurt, Ella.'

'Why should I be? I've had a lovely time,' she replied, looking for her clutch bag. He handed it to her.

'Here.' Next moment, he was jumping out and coming round the front of the vehicle. She sat, feeling numb. Her head understood it all well enough, but her body didn't! It had wanted so much more after that kiss.

He opened the door and she sat still for a moment, then turned to get out. This time he wasn't looking at her legs, but only into her eyes. 'Costas may come on the trip,' he said. 'I know you will look after him.'

'Thank you.' She felt so happy that he trusted her.

'Oh, I forgot, the car's ready and my friend's delivering it to me. Would you like me to come and fetch you to get it — and then you can see Costas.'

'I'd love that,' she said. He smiled and the tension between the two of them seemed to lift.

'Tomorrow?'

'I think I can make it,' she said.

'I'm glad. I didn't know whether you would want to see me again.'

'Of course I do.' She smiled thinking it had been such a *little boy* thing to say, at the time wondering how situations can change in seconds. It was as if their encounter had never happened.

'Until tomorrow then. Come on, I'll see you up the drive. You know, June should get it widened and then neither of you would have to walk to the door.' Everything between them seemed mundane, but Ella was determined to hold those earlier moments in her heart.

Two seconds later, he took her hand and kissed it. She fluttered inside at the touch of his lips again. Then straightening, Loukas kissed her on both cheeks like the Greeks do naturally. They could have been only the slightest of friends. '*Ya sou,* Ella,' he said.

'*Ya sou,* Loukas.'

'Tomorrow then?' he said.

'Tomorrow.' He watched as Ella took out her key and opened the door. Then with a quick wave, he was striding away down the drive. She stood there and watched him drive away. As soon as she opened the door, June came out of the kitchen. She had a mug in her hand and was still in her dressing gown.

'I know I'm nosy,' she said, 'but how did it go?' If Ella had been herself she would have been only too glad to chat.

'Let's say . . . It went as well as expected.'

'I'm sorry, love. Would you like a drink?'

Ella couldn't bear the I-told-you-so look on her friend's face. She sighed. 'No, thank you, but I promise I'll tell you all about it in the morning.'

'Goodnight then,' replied June, 'Sleep tight.' A moment later, Ella had disappeared. Poor kid, thought June as she followed behind. But I'm not surprised. Not at all.

CHAPTER 6

The morning didn't come quickly
enough for Ella, because she was seeing Loukas again.

'So you're meeting him today?'
asked June. 'I'm surprised as I got
the impression something had gone
wrong last night.'

'I was just tired.' Although she loved
June, Ella didn't feel able to tell her
what had happened to upset her.
'Nothing was wrong. We had a lovely
time.' She related how marvellous the
venue and the meal had been and
was most relieved when June seemed

satisfied.

Later, as Ella walked down the drive with Loukas she was thinking about the evening before, and wondered if he felt the same, but no sign was apparent. He had greeted her in the most pleasant way and the drive up to his house was uneventful, chatting about trivialities.

However, she was met at the door by Costas with an enthusiasm that even surprised her. Anna was collecting her things as they entered, with Costas holding Ella's hand and chatting away about his newest toy. Even Ella felt sorry for her as she said goodbye, thinking it must have been galling for the girl, who fixed her with a hostile stare.

'Bye, Anna,' called Loukas, then turned to Ella. 'Coffee?'

'Please.' Ella sat down and Costas ran to her and sat on her lap.

'Off,' said Loukas. 'You're a bit too heavy for Ella.'

'Can I bring my book then?' asked his son, looking disappointed. Ella was sorry for the little boy, but didn't say anything. After all, it wasn't her business. But then Loukas relented.

'Fetch your book then, but you can't sit on Ella's knee.' Costas trotted off, returned and handed her a book. As she and Costas began to read, she took the advantage of saying,

'Did you teach him to read, Loukas?' she asked as he was bringing over her coffee.

'Of course.'

'He's very forward. For his age.'

'Why? He's six.' Costas gave him a

sideways look. 'Sorry, Costas, six and a half.' The little boy smiled.

"But this is a difficult book.'

'He's smart. He takes after me.' Loukas' grin was infectious. They all laughed and once more the tension was broken. He turned to Costas, 'Enough reading for now. Here's your drink. I suggest you go out and play for a bit. Ella and I have things to discuss.' Costas made a face, but did as he was told.

'He's very good,' praised Ella.

'I've tried to bring him up properly, but . . .'

'Well, you've done a good job. I have a *but* too, Loukas. Doesn't he have any playmates?'

'He doesn't need them.'

'I think . . .'

'We go into town quite often.' She

151

could see Loukas was on the defensive and she didn't want to say something that would dispel his good mood. I shouldn't be tip-toeing round him like this, thought Ella. Why am I doing it? 'Anyway,' he added, 'I've told him he's going out with you.' She was shocked for a moment.

'There'll be other children there and I hope he'll make some friends, even though it's only for a day,' she said, formulating her plan and evidently succeeding.

'So, as you've evidently made a hit, I can leave him in your hands. I'm not going, I'm afraid. Would you be able to pick him up on the way if I fetch him from the site?' She nodded, amazed again he was being so accommodating and also trusting

Costas to her. Ella thought how June would react to that.

'I'm flattered,' she said.

'No, you're a teacher. You're meant to look after your charges.' She assumed the reproof was only in fun.

'I'd look after him anyway.' She looked directly at him — and he didn't avoid her gaze.

'I know — and I think of you . . .' He hesitated. She felt a little throb inside.

'How do you think of me, Loukas?' she appealed.

'As a friend. As . . . someone I . . .' She put out her hand and touched his arm.

'I feel that way too, you know.'

'I advise you not to, Ella. You don't know me.'

'What do you mean?'

'I'm hopeless with women.' She was shocked again.

'What makes you say that?' What she really wanted to say was, You loved your wife and, now, you could love somebody again. I know you could. But she didn't. She felt to take the initiative with him would be a mistake, because he might rebuff her, and she couldn't bear the thought. 'Anyway, I'm sure that's not true. Anna is evidently very fond of you.'

'Is that what you think? Anna is only here because . . .' He broke off. 'I don't want to talk about Anna.'

'What a puzzle he is,' thought Ella. He sounded as if he didn't even like the girl. If so, why was she working for him? Why did he let his precious son be looked after by her? What was the mystery?

'I won't ask why,' she said, 'because it isn't my business.' She sighed. 'When is your friend bringing the car?'

'Oh, it's here already. In one of the outhouses. I put it away because I wasn't sure whether you'd come to fetch it after last night.'

'Of course I would,' she said. To hear him mention last night was a huge relief, that washed over her, making her heart beat faster. 'What about last night?'

'I went too far.'

'You didn't,' she said. 'You only kissed me.' He was close to her now. She looked through the open window at Costas who was playing in his sandpit.

'He's all right,' he said. 'Don't worry it won't happen again.'

How could she tell him she wanted it to? But she didn't want to hear how devoted he still was to Xanthe.

'Believe me I'm not worried about it.' The moment passed. What's the matter with me, she thought. Why can't I tell him how I feel? *Maybe you're in love with him,* came an unexpected little voice from deep within her. Was it possible that she had fallen for a man she couldn't even talk to; who was unable even to speak of his past. She should walk away now, before it was too late. Was he truly sorry that he "went too far."

'Shall we talk about Costas now,' she asked, thinking how wonderful it would be if we could be as open and honest as his son was, who showed emotion without question. 'You said you trust me. How would you feel if

I asked you to let him go to school properly? I'd look after him.' She waited for the reaction.

'I wish I could,' he said.

'It's a lovely school — and I know he would make friends. He's such a sweet little boy.'

'Let's start with this trip,' he said, 'and see how he gets on.'

'Thank you.' Ella hoped her relief was not too evident. A moment later, he caught her arm. She looked down, then up into his face.

'Why are you so interested in Costas, Ella?'

'Because I think that . . . he needs more than you, Loukas!' The words came out before Ella could stop herself.

'What you're trying to say is — that he needs a mother.' His grip hard-

157

ened and Ella was alarmed at the effect her words had produced.

'I wouldn't presume to say anything like that,' she said. 'Not even think it.' His grip relaxed.

'I'm sorry,' he said. 'I didn't want to upset you. I hope I haven't hurt you.' He was looking at her arm. 'I wouldn't want to do that.'

'I know,' she replied. Somehow, someone had to say something! Was she brave enough? She plunged in. 'I can imagine how you feel. Really, I can. You must miss her a lot.' She swallowed.

'What do you know about it, Ella?' She could see sadness now, not anger.

'Only what June told me. That you lost Xanthe in an accident.'

'You even know her name.'

'Yes,' replied Ella in a voice that

would hardly come out. She knew that she shouldn't have mentioned his wife. 'It must have been terrible for you.'

'It was. In a way. You've been brave to offer your condolences, but, Ella, you know nothing about us. How we were.'

'I'm sorry. I didn't mean to pry.' Of course, they had been deeply in love — and she never had.

'You have nothing to be sorry about. I am protective of Costas because of the things that have happened."

'I'm sure nothing will happen to him, Loukas, if you let him go.'

'That's very philosophical, but I'm afraid I have a different view. Presumably, your friend, June, didn't fill in all the gaps. So please don't ask me to.'

'I've offended you.'

'No, I'm not offended. I just regret that I've wasted so many years of my life and Costas' too.'

'Not wasted,' Ella said. 'It'll be all right. Honestly.' She felt so sad for him and also ashamed to sound like some insincere character in a Hollywood movie, telling someone who was seriously injured that "everything was going to be all right." And it never was.

'Can we change the subject, please?' he asked.

'Yes. I think you should get the car out.' replied Ella. She felt that at last she'd managed to get somewhere. There was a long way to go yet, but she was willing to try. A few minutes later, hand-in-hand with Costas chattering on about his toys, she stood watching Loukas back out her car. It looked as good as new. And she had thought it would be a write-off. Loukas' friend was evidently not only quick, but also knew what he was doing.

Loukas wound down the window. 'Don't worry. I've checked it over. And he's good at his job. It looked worse than it was.'

'I trust you,' she said — and he smiled as he got out. 'Thank you for seeing to the car. When shall I pay?'

'No problem. He'll send the bill to the Vialla Agios.' They were standing very close and he looked near to kissing her again, but with a glance down at Costas, he added, 'We'll see you soon.'

'When?' asked Costas, his face creased into something between a smile and a tear.

'You're going out with Ella and I'm fetching you back.'

'When, when?' Costas jumped up and down, then stopped as his father looked at him.

'So I'll pick him up on the way and then you'll fetch him from the site — that's if you haven't changed your mind about coming for the whole day.'

'Sorry. Would you like Ella to pick you up?' he asked his son, who was again hopping about in excitement.

'Yes. I want to go with her.'

'You've certainly made a hit with him, and . . .' he hesitated.

'Don't worry, I understand.' She got into the car. 'I'll let you know the full programme when I come, but pick up at the site will be no later than three. I'm so happy you agreed.'

'So am I,' he answered quite unexpectedly. As Ella drove away and waved, she could see them through the back window. Both were standing side by side, watching, the small boy hanging on to his tall father's hand. Her heart went out to them. They were so lonely! Inside, Ella was feeling a kind of happiness she could truly say she had never felt before and, and that moment, it all seemed to be right in her world, even though the shadow of his lost wife was everpresent. She only hoped that Loukas felt the same.

When she got back to the villa and parked, she ran in and found the place empty. June must have gone shopping, so she took the unwelcome opportunity to ring Takis, knowing the sooner she obtained more details the better. She was still feeling miffed. Usually, the teacher should be the one who made the decisions about her pupils, but in this case, she had to admit Takis was in a better position than she was to arrange such things in the school holidays and to persuade the villagers that a trip out of school time had some value, as even the youngest were expected to be out in the fields, helping their parents. She lifted the handset.

'Takis, I thought I should ring you for more details of the trip.'

'Ella, what a pleasure. I was going to ring you.' His voice was fluid and complimentary.

'I need to know how many children are going and the firm arrangements.'

'I have organised this already. We shall be taking a bus. The driver is a friend of mine.'

'How many are coming?'

'Fifteen and several parents — and of course, I shall be there.' She wrote down all the details. Yes, he knew how to do a good job, but he was so smooth it made her feel sick.

'I would love to see you before.'

'I'm afraid that's impossible, Takis. I have *so* much work to do.'

'Very well.' She could tell he had taken offence by the tone of his voice. 'But I am looking forward to my day with you very much,' he added.

I'm not, thought Ella. Her reply was non-committal. She replaced the handset and stared at it as if it was about to crawl away.

'You seemed a bit cool. Was that Takis?' asked June, coming through with her shopping bags.

'Unfortunately. He was giving me the details of the trip. I didn't want him to ring me.'

'You want to watch him,' said June.

'Don't worry, I shall, but I have some very interesting news. In fact . . .' Her eyes lit up.

'It must be about Loukas,' replied June. 'You wouldn't look like that about anyone else.'

'Loukas is letting Costas come with me on the trip!' June stared at her.

'I can't believe it. What did you do?'

'I just asked him.'

'You're a miracle-worker. And — very sexy!'

'June!'

'If you can get under Loukas' skin, then you really must be something.' The older woman nodded, making her outrageous earrings jangle even more. 'Now, I'm worn out from shopping, so let's go and sit by the pool and cool off.'

'I'll make some iced tea,' replied Ella, laughing.

On the day of the trip, Ella drove towards the house on the mountain. Even the early morning was oppressively hot and the news was full of several fires breaking out on the other side of the island. The thought of the lovely forests being reduced to burnt sticks made Ella sick. However, when she arrived, she was cheered up by the sight of Costas, who was already hopping around on the doorstep, a small knapsack on his back and a sun hat on his head. He rushed towards Ella, shouting, 'Daddy. She's here!' A second later, Loukas was outside too. He looked as great in jeans as the Italian suit. But his face was drawn and he had dark circles under his eyes as if he'd been out all night.

'He's been driving me mad since the early hours,' he said.

'I can imagine, and he'll be fine.' She could detect a note of anxiety in Loukas' demeanour. 'I'll keep him with me. I promise.'

'Thank you.' The little boy was running towards the car. 'Be good, Costas. Be careful, Ella.'

'I will.' She knew what he meant and how important it was that he should hear her promise. She was about to turn when he caught hold of her arm.

'I really mean it,' he said. She gasped. For a moment, she thought he was going to kiss her. They stood very close, facing each other. Then Costas laughed out loud, breaking into the silence, and Ella caught the sight of Anna hovering in the doorway. Ella didn't know whether to feel embarrassed or triumphant. Instead, she felt a tiny bit uneasy. Had the girl been staying there all night? Then she decided that wasn't fair. She'd said she trusted him. *Are you jealous,* asked the little voice in her head?

'Here you are, Loukas.' Trying to cover her confusion, Ella rummaged in her bag, searching for a copy of all the day's itinerary. She handed it to him. 'We'll see you at the site about three?'

'I'll be there,' he nodded. Moments later, having belted Costas in safely, she started the engine and made her way up the path on to the mountain road. She looked into the mirror and could see Loukas, standing, watching them.

The little boy was waving wildly to his father. As they rounded the bend where she'd had the accident, he turned to her, his dark eyes wide and pleading. 'Are we there yet, Ella?'

The minibus carrying her small pupils and some parents parked outside the ancient site. At that moment, although having experienced such excitement on the bus, Ella wondered if this had been a good idea. A nature walk on the beach might have been better. But it hadn't been her idea to bring them, but that of Takis, whom she suspected had decided it was the only way to get her on his own for some length of time.

She had managed *not* to sit by him on the bus and he had glared at Costas, which disgusted Ella so much that she glared back at him, which had no effect because he returned the scathing glance with a grin. However Costas didn't seem to notice or hopefully if he did, he didn't understand. Doubtless he was used to Anna's scowls!

Two other small boys sat opposite them and soon he was chatting away. Ella was surprised to see how confident Costas was. This pointed once more to the fact Loukas was doing a good job bringing up his son. It could have been very different.

However, all the children were well-behaved and those parents who had come with them had been most respectful to her as the teacher and most obliging. In fact, it was quite unnerving. They listened very carefully as Ella explained the history of the place in a manner that small children understood and which drew compliments from the adults. Then she let her pupils explore the ruins, which turned out to be very exciting and left a lot of red dust on their clothes! She was feeling happy she'd done a good job when the parents took over, each supervising a little group of their own for lunch.

The only thing spoiling the day for Ella, was Takis. He wouldn't leave her alone, behaving as if they were the best of friends — and more. She felt embarrassed and annoyed, especially in front of the adults. Even when she joined a group of them, pointing out various things that might interest small children and telling them the old stories, Takis had been very close behind her.

About half an hour before they were ready to leave, they were all sitting beneath the olive trees having a cool drink. The wind was sharp now, cooling the heat of the afternoon as it swirled across the surface of the aquamarine sea. The site was high on the cliff top and if you looked far below, it was stirring the waves into flecks of boiling foam. Its unkind touch had fashioned the ancient trees making them misshapen like bent old men and danced and twisted over the sandy earth, whipping it up into unsuspecting small eyes, which not even the kindly shelter of the trees could avoid. Even then, Ella couldn't feel comfortable because Takis was still trying it on.

I can't bear this harassment any more, thought Ella. In the end, I'll have to tell him! But her job might be on the line, if she mentioned this inappropriate behaviour to any of the other governors. Although Takis' family was one of the most important in the area, she suspected it wasn't popular after things she had heard, but she didn't doubt there were many girls who would look at his handsome face and be happy to succumb to his charms. He looked so suave that day in his designer jeans — and he knew it!

Then she thought of Loukas whom

she had seen earlier, who looked worn out and tired. How different his life was from Takis' shallow existence, whose determination to pursue Ella probably came from the thrill of chasing her. As a chauvinist, Takis couldn't understand that any woman he approached didn't fall at his feet. Ella had known already she thoroughly disliked him, but now she couldn't stand him any more.

'Takis, *please,*' she said moving away, as he attempted to put his arm around her in front of everyone.

'Why don't you like me, Ella,' he whispered close in her ear, as if he were her lover.

'It's not that . . .' She was struggling for the right way of saying what she meant, without being openly rude, '. . . that I don't *like* you,' she lied, 'but you are behaving in-appropriately.' She looked across to the other adults in the party.

'Ah, you are worried about *them,*' he said dismissively, gesturing to-wards a small group of parents who had moved further away, possibly because they didn't want to spoil things for her. 'Take no notice. Most of them are peasants!' Ella was shocked at his arrogance. He was close again. 'Does this mean that if I was behaving *appropriately* I would have a chance?'

'*No!* If you don't stop, I shall go over and join them.' She had an urge to slap him. His behaviour was un-bearable.

'You have spirit,' replied Takis, look-ing at her approvingly. 'I like that.' He was impossible. At that moment, she was wishing she had never taken the teaching post. She closed her bottle of squash with a snap. Why should he spoil things for her?

'I have my pupils to see to.' She looked over at Costas talking in an animated way to one of his new friends.

'Why did you bring the boy?' asked Takis. In a second, his tone had changed from fluidly complimentary to accusing.

'Because I thought he would like it. And he deserves to be at school. Isn't that what you want too?'

'He will be a troublemaker like his father.'

'No, I think it is you who are making the trouble.' She was so angry again that he should turn on a child.

'Excuse me?' he scowled.

'Just why don't you want that little boy to come to school?' she snapped. 'He's having a marvellous time. What is your reason for disliking him and his father so much?'

'I told you — he's a troublemaker.' He avoided her question with skill. Several parents were staring now and then one of them said something in a whisper and they all laughed. Ella went red. She was not given to blushing, but she'd had enough. Doubtless, they thought she and Takis were having a lover's tiff. She put as much distance between the two of them as she could and said,

'Well, if he is such a problem to you, why is your cousin Anna working for Loukas?' He didn't answer. 'Anyway, your problem will be solved soon. I've decided that if I can't get

Costas back into school for whatever reason, I shall visit his house in my own time and give him private lessons. That won't be illegal as I'm a certificated teacher.' It was the first time she had seen Takis shocked, or at least with nothing to say. A moment later, she walked off and beckoned Costas, who came running over with his friends.

'We're not going are we, Ella? Please!'

'Not quite yet, Costas,' she said, consulting her watch. 'You and your friends can come with me to the shop and we'll buy something for your daddy.' Costas looked very happy. She did not offer ice cream as she might be seen as having favourites, but she longed to let her little charge indulge. She thought I don't even know if his daddy has ever taken him out and bought him ice cream. Maybe the three of us can go together one day . . . It was a lovely thought. 'But before that I need to tell everyone that we only have another twenty minutes before we have to go back to the minibus.' The children made a face, but waited patiently until she finished organising the rest of the party. Soon the parents were collecting their children and making their way to either the shop or the gates.

As they walked to the entrance with Takis trailing behind them, Ella looked at Costas' happy little face and was determined to let Loukas know once more what his son was missing by having no playmates. She looked at her watch again. It was ten to three. Suddenly she was hoping Loukas would be on time. She knew nothing about his punctuality. If he wasn't, what would she do?

Inside the shop, they looked at everything. She found some attractive jewellery and handled it, then put it back. Costas settled on a key ring.

'Do you think he will like it, Ella?'

'I'm sure he will. It's very pretty.'

'Like you.'

'Thank you, Costas,' she said, bending down, 'but you shouldn't say that. I am your teacher.'

'But it's true,' he said. 'Will you always be my teacher, Ella?'

'I hope so, Costas,' she replied, smiling. 'Now we should go and look for your daddy.' She turned round and nearly ran into Takis. She avoided him as quickly as she could but he was still behind her. Costas was running ahead, as they came out of the shop. To her horror, Takis slipped his arm around her waist and whispered in her ear,

'I could buy you better jewellery than that cheap stuff.' She was about to break away, when she looked across and saw Loukas sitting in the 4×4, watching them! He had a set expression on his face. Ella was horrified. The last thing she wanted was for him to see her with Takis.

'Leave me alone,' she said and he let her go. Loukas was walking towards them. He was wearing the fireman's jacket, with flashes on it. He must have been working. Ella caught her breath. He was so handsome, but now Takis had spoiled *everything*. By then, Costas had seen his father and was running towards him shouting. She saw Loukas smile briefly at his son.

'Loukas,' she called and walked towards him — with Takis still in tow. When she got near, she saw the look on Loukas' grim face. It was almost as if he didn't know her. 'You're early.'

'Like you, I had things to do.' The pointed remark didn't escape her, or surprisingly because Costas, who had been standing by Loukas, sidled over to her and took her hand. His father stared at him. 'Come here and say thank you to the teacher, Costas.'

'Thank you, Ella.'

'I'm glad you had a lovely time, Costas. I did,' she said, bending down and shaking his hand.

'And so did I,' interrupted Takis,

grinning at Ella. He's so vile, she thought. He knows exactly what he's doing. The two men stared at each other.

'Takis,' said Loukas. The hostility between them was evident. Ella was worried and she could see the occupants of the bus staring at them. It really was too bad that she had been put in this position. She should never have agreed to go with Takis.

'I think you should take your son home,' replied Takis and Ella gasped.

'Only too pleased,' growled Loukas. 'Come on, Costas.'

'Bye, Ella,' shouted the little boy as his father pulled him along towards the 4x4.

'Up you get!' said Loukas and Ella watched Costas scramble into the vehicle. She stood there — with Takis still beside her. There was nothing she could do. Thoughts were rushing through her head. Loukas must think she and Takis were together . . . She couldn't bear it. Now, he'd never let Costas go to school.

'Loukas?' she called, hurrying over to the vehicle.

'Thank you for inviting Costas,' he answered. His voice was distant. 'But I've somewhere to be.' She could see all he wanted to do was to get away. A moment later he was in the driving seat and switching on the ignition. She watched as she saw him fiddling with Costas' seat belt. As he lifted his head, he looked straight at her. She couldn't have described the look on his face. Was it regret, sadness, or even loathing? Evidently he hated Takis as much as she did and was classing her as the same sort of person! A moment later, he backed the vehicle away and drove off, stirring the dust into a red cloud. She looked round at Takis, who appeared to be enjoying the scene immensely.

'Don't ever do that again,' her anger spilled out.

'Do what?' he shrugged.

'You know what I mean!' Ella marched off towards the minibus. What should have been a beautiful day was ruined. And her plans for a lonely little boy had been destroyed. As for her dreams . . . At that moment, she hated Takis!

CHAPTER 7

On the journey back, Ella put her bag on her seat, now she had no one sitting beside her, in case Takis decided to. No way, she thought and again he was forced to sit in the same seat he had occupied on the way there. A light breeze was blowing, dispelling the punishing heat of day, as the minibus finally arrived in the village square. Several of the smallest children had been fast asleep and were very grumpy when they woke up, some of them sobbing and grizzling. Ella knew how they felt.

As they alighted, the village was lit up by a dark red sun sinking behind the summits of the surrounding mountains, leaving a warm glow behind, reddening the quaint roofs and buttering the old stones of the houses. But that late afternoon, Ella did not appreciate the beauty around her.

As the parents thanked her and shook her hand, she listened to their compliments in a haze, with her brain computing how she could put things right with Loukas. Deep inside, she felt that whatever excuse she gave might not convince him. She needed to know what had happened in the past between the two men, but now she didn't care if only she could restore his trust.

On the other hand, she realised he

was jealous, which must have meant something, although as far as Ella was concerned, jealousy was not a cause for rejoicing. Perhaps Costas would tell him she and Takis had been together all day, but she couldn't imagine Loukas would let his little son get involved by questioning him. How can I make it up to him, she thought. How can I make him believe me that I couldn't get rid of Takis; that I feel nothing for that creep.

Takis had been watching the good-byes and nodding to the parents in a self-satisfied way as if he were the one they should have been thanking for his marvellous idea. As the last child and his mother finished talking to her, Ella was ready to run — but he was after her and caught her up unlocking her car.

'Don't dare to say anything to me!' On rare occasions, Ella lost her temper, but when she did, according to her father, she wasn't sensible and he'd added, "in fact, rather dangerous!" On one occasion, she had thrown her dinner across the room and been sent to bed in disgrace.

'You look lovely when you're angry,' Takis replied.

'Don't! Or I might do something I'll regret.' She struggled to stay calm. 'Never, ever, ask me to go out with you again. Now, *go away!*'

Takis was grinning as she got into her car and slammed the door. A moment later, she accelerated so hard that a heap of books she'd brought with her and intended to put into the school room when she had arrived in the morning, shot off the back seat and on to the floor.

By then, the sensible voice inside her was winning. On the outskirts of the village when she had put some space between her and Takis, she slowed down. It was a dangerous road! Besides, she had an idea. She had to pass the house on the mountain and — as her plan became clearer — she decided to call in on Loukas. It would be better to get things out in the open, rather than let them fester. She squinted at the clock on the dashboard display. Loukas would have been back for over an hour by now and probably he'd cooled off, like she had. Maybe she could explain.

Mindful of the hairpins, she swung Hermie down the mountain road.

June would have said she was driving too fast, but now Ella's mind was made up, she had to get it over with. Whatever happened between them would make her feel better than she did now and also she had to argue her case for Costas' future happiness.

She could see the house already and had turned into the drive when she realised the 4x4 was not parked outside. He was out! No, she thought, he's probably put the vehicle round the back for the night. I'm going to try anyway. Although she was fixed on what she was was going to say, she couldn't help noticing the row of lovely terracotta pots, their inhabitants spilling petals over on to the pebbles. He even liked the same flowers as she did . . . As she reached the door and was about to knock, it opened to reveal Anna!

'What are you doing here?' asked the girl. She was wearing only a towel, knotted at the breasts. Her hair was wet through. 'I'm showering.'

'I've come to see Loukas,' retorted Ella. 'And Costas.' She couldn't help thinking about Anna stepping out of her clothes and going into the shower, naked, and Loukas . . .

'You're journey's wasted. Neither of them are here. In fact, they've gone away.'

'Gone away?' Disappointment rose inside Ella, almost choking her. 'But . . . But I was talking to them only about an hour ago. Loukas didn't mention it.' The nasty little voice in her head said, *Are you surprised?*

'Why should he? He planned it ages

ago.' The girl looked triumphant. 'You can go away now, I'm busy.'

'I can see that! Where has he gone?'

'Why do you want to know?'

'I do. We have business to discuss. And you only work here.'

'Well, you'll be unlucky then,' Anna replied nastily. 'If you really want to know, he's gone to another island. To relatives.'

'When will he be back?'

'I only work here,' snapped the girl and slammed the door in her face. At that moment, Ella was near to crying. In fact, it really brought the tears to her eyes as she remembered how Loukas had carried her into the house; how his apparent anger had changed to tenderness; how close they had become. 'Well, almost close,' she sniffed as she walked over to her car. 'And now, I've blown it,' she said out loud as she got into Hermie. She was too upset to drive for a moment, but then she recovered. Why hadn't he told her he planned to go away? Maybe it was because of what had happened when he'd seen her and Takis together. Don't flatter yourself, she thought. He'd planned it already probably and he didn't care enough to tell you. Anyway, why should he tell her? He could do what he liked, both on his own account and his son's.

She tried to remember exactly what he'd said to her when she'd asked if Costas could go on the trip. It came back to her with a sharp stab that was truly painful. "I've wasted my own life as well as Costas," which was a dreadful thing to say. Before that he'd said he was hopeless with women. Whatever did that mean? And now he'd gone to relatives on another island without telling her! It was a good thing that June hadn't been there to see Ella drive down the mountain in a haze of tears. All she wanted then was to get back to the villa and allow herself to be truly miserable!

'I'm so glad to see you, Ella,' cried June. Ella looked at her. She was still in a daze.

'Why? What's the matter?' A sudden hope came to her. 'You haven't seen Loukas?'

'No. Should I have? What do you mean? Didn't he allow Costas to go as promised?' June was looking at her.

'Yes, he kept his promise, but . . .'

'You don't appear to have had a very good time. All right. I won't pry.'

Ella sniffled. 'I'm all right. I'm just tired. Anyway, why were you so glad to see me. I'm not *that* late.'

'I suppose you haven't been listening to the news. The fires have spread to us. To Rhodes. Isn't it terrible? I've been worried sick. But, then, I got sensible and realised you were going in the other direction.'

'Slow down, June.' Ella put a soothing hand on June's shoulder. 'Tell me properly.'

'I've just seen it on television. The forest fires. They're here. And I was thinking we'd avoided them. I'd like to kill whoever started them. Lighting matches. Smoking!'

'Where exactly are the fires?' asked Ella. The day seemed to have gone very cold.

'They're all around us really. On other islands. And now we have them.'

'Other islands?' Ella's stomach turned over.

'Yes, they've stopped the ferries.'

'So people can't get off?'

'Not at present. Why? Were you thinking of going somewhere?'

'No,' replied Ella, thinking hard. So probably Loukas didn't go at all. He would have known how dangerous it was. And that's why he was wearing that jacket when he picked up Costas. That was what he had to do. Helping with the fires. So Anna must have been lying!

'I wish I was leaving,' said June. 'I'm frightened of the fire coming and taking all this.'

'No, it won't,' replied Ella, hoping she sounded convincing.

'Anyway, why did you ask if I'd seen Loukas? He's bound to be out there fighting it.'

'You think so?'

'I know so,' June said, 'He's dedicated to his job — when he does it. He cares about his house and the forests as much as I care about all this here. It's only volunteers like Loukas who can get together and stop it.'

'Does he have relatives on another island, June?'

'No, but he has an elderly great aunt, who lives next to my Dimitri's cousin,' said June. 'That's where I hear all . . .' She broke off.

'The gossip?'

'I'm afraid so. Awful, isn't it?'

'You know all about Loukas, don't you, June?'

'I'm sorry, Ella, but it isn't my place. He has to tell you himself,' replied June. She looked upset. Ella laid a hand on her friend's arm.

'No, it's me that should be sorry. Do you know the great aunt's number?'

'I'm not sure if she's even on the phone. Has something happened to Loukas and Costas?'

'I called on the way down the mountain and when I got to the house, Anna said . . .' June frowned. '. . . Said that he'd taken Costas to another island to be with relatives.'

'He hasn't any, except in the village. Of course, he may have *friends* on other islands, but I don't know of any . . . Besides, he wouldn't go now,' said June, 'not with these fires. He loves this island. His roots are here. That Anna, you can't believe a word she says. No, Loukas often takes Costas to see his great aunt. She's the only one of Loukas' father's family that is left. Nice woman. That's where he will have taken him, so he can get on with the job. What's going on, Ella?'

'I can't tell you now,' she replied, 'but if that girl has been telling lies, I'll . . .'

'She'll be sorry!' It was good to see June smile.

'Yes,' replied Ella.

'I know what. I'll ring up and see what my friend has to say.'

'Oh, would you?'

'Anything to put a smile on that pretty face,' answered June.

'You're so good to me.' Ella sat down. She felt quite weak all of a sudden.

'And then we'll have a cup of real English tea. Now, where's that phone?'

'Will you do something for me?' asked Ella suddenly as June picked up the handset.

'Of course,' replied June.

'If Costas *is* there, could you try and find out when Loukas is fetching him home. I *have* to speak to him.'

'Oh, dear,' said June, 'I don't know what's gone wrong, but I can't believe you want to go back up the mountain. It's too dangerous."

'You don't know what happened.'

'Sorry! I'm a meddling old woman. I'm sure you'll tell me in your own good time.'

June was right! Costas had been delivered to his great aunt and the villagers were already packing up their essential belongings just in case the fire got as far as the mountain. 'But that's highly unlikely,' June explained, 'because so high above the forest there's only sparse vegetation, except for the vines. Now, about picking up Costas. According to my cousin-in-law, Loukas is going to fetch Costas back home around noon tomorrow. But that will depend on the state of the fires. I can see what you're thinking, Ella, but whatever has happened between you two, you mustn't go up there. It isn't safe. Besides, he wouldn't dream of picking up Costas if it wasn't. So you can't be sure where he'll be. Please don't even think about going!'

'Look, June,' Ella sighed, 'I know you want to do what you think's best for me, but I don't intend to take any chances.' June looked relieved. 'However . . . I *am* going to go . . . But only as far as Loukas' house.'

'No!' June almost shouted.

'Will you ask your cousin to go round to the aunt and say that the schoolteacher needs to speak to Loukas urgently. That she'll be at his house at midday. If he doesn't turn up, then I'll come home.'

'It's too risky! I won't do it!'

'*Please.* What if — something happened to Loukas and I'd never told him . . .' She broke off.

'That you loved him? Is that what you were going to say, Ella?'

'I beg you to do this. For me?'

June stared at Ella. 'If I promise, what shall I do if something happens to you.'

'It won't! I've more sense than that. I shall only go as far as the house — and only if it's safe. At any hint of fire, I'll come back. It's not a million miles away is it?'

'It seems like it to me.'

'*Please*, June!'

June sighed and pressed her lips together. 'Did anyone ever tell you, you were stubborn.'

'Yes, especially my father.'

'Well, I could add to that. He should have said *foolhardy!*' She breathed in deeply. 'All right, I'll do it, but it's breaking my heart. We'll keep an eye on the news and if, by any chance, the fires have spread in that direction, you promise you won't go?'

'I promise. Thank you, June. You've saved my life.' Ella kissed her on the cheek. The older woman half-smiled, then the expression was replaced by the most serious Ella had ever seen on June's face.

'I hope there'll be someone to save *your* life, if the wind changes. Doubtless Loukas will tell you that, if he turns up. I'm sure that he'll get your message. I know something else too. That he'll be angry. Phew!' June fanned herself. 'Now, let's go and have that cuppa. Or would you prefer a cold drink?'

Ella could see that she'd upset June, but something inside told her she had to go to Loukas, angry or not. Just in case she never saw him again!

Early the following morning Ella thought of nothing else but her impending trip and was tortured by the possibility that the great aunt might not give Loukas the message. She and June had been watching the progress of the fires carefully. Although they were now blazing away on the foothills of neighbouring mountains, they were not near theirs.

'I wish you wouldn't go,' pleaded June, as they sat by the pool. 'You've heard of the expression "like wildfire" I suppose? These fires spread in a few hours!'

'I know what you're trying to tell me, but please don't worry. I'm a big girl.'

'If you were my daughter, I

wouldn't let you go,' retorted June.

'You're lovely, but I shall be okay.'
Ella put her hand on June's arm. At
that moment they heard a car pull
up outside. They stared at each other.

'Please God, it's Loukas!" said
June.

'I don't think so,' replied Ella.
Unfortunately, she was right. By the
time they were on their feet, they
heard knocking.

'I'll go,' said Ella. She made for the
door with June behind, and opened
it quickly. 'You!'

'Don't slam the door in my face,'
said Takis. He put one foot on the
step, looking contrite. But it didn't
fool Ella. 'I've been thinking about
what you said,' he added.

'What? That I never wanted to see
you again!' She couldn't remember

actually saying *that,* but somewhere near. She heard June clear her throat and turned. 'It's all right, June, I'm handling this.'

'If you'll let me in, I'll explain.'

'The step will do,' she said. June was beside her now.

'It's about Loukas.' Ella was shocked.

'Maybe you should let him in,' said June unexpectedly.

'Thank you,' he said. Ella was surprised. She knew how much June disliked him.

'What's going on?' asked Ella. Takis looked away. June winked.

'All right, come in,' said Ella, standing back.

'You should go in the dining room,' added June. 'But let me go first and check everything's tidy.' Ella could see June was up to something. The room was always spotless. They waited in the hallway without speaking and she noticed Takis couldn't resist looking into the mirror and smoothing back his hair She grimaced.

When June came out, she said, 'I'll be in the kitchen, if you need me.' Ella knew June meant she'd be at the ready if the situation became awkward, but she still didn't know why her friend had agreed to let him in.

'Right,' said Ella, looking at her watch. 'Come along, but I can't give you much of my time.' She realised she sounded like a schoolteacher and that was how it was going to be. Business.

They sat on the ornately carved chairs, facing each other, but with a good distance between them. The room was cool, but Ella felt far from that, although she promised herself she wouldn't lose her temper. Still, *he looks as though he's sorry for being so horrible,* she thought. *Maybe he's taken the hint at last?*

'Well?' she asked. 'You said it was about Loukas. *And* I'm expecting an apology.'

'You have it,' he said. 'I might have gone too far — but you're very attractive.' His eyes strafed her body, which wasn't an encouraging start.

'I am only interested in talking business,' she replied. 'I hope it's something about school and Costas. Otherwise, I don't want to hear.' She did really, especially if he was going to explain about the enmity between the two men.

'It's exactly that,' he replied. 'The business of Costas and Loukas.'

'Oh.' She was surprised. 'Carry on.'

'I've been looking up the rules about home schooling,' he began. 'Public education is mandatory here and the practice is illegal.' He sounded like a textbook.

'Well, I know several people who do it quite openly.' She was determined to put him off the scent, even though she already knew what he said was true that it was illegal.

'I'm not talking about ex-pats, but citizens. As I told you some time ago, I have been looking into it. Loukas Milas is committing a crime.'

'A crime?'

'For which he could be prosecuted.' He sat back. Ella's colour rose.

'Is that what you've come to tell

me?' You intend to prosecute him.'

'Partially. Of course it would be at the discretion of the school governors to make any decision about criminality.'

'And you are the Chairman.' In spite of the heat rising within her, Ella's voice was cold. 'Have you come here to threaten me, Takis?' She could hear June in the kitchen and suspected she was listening at the door. Maybe she should have asked her in to be a witness?

'Our discretion would be based on several matters. Maybe this problem could be overlooked on compassionate grounds, but another cannot. If you wish to keep your own job, I advise you strongly that you should not think of involving yourself with this child's education — nor with this man. It would be dangerous and naturally I, personally, would not like to see that happen. It might prejudice your position.'

'Or?' asked Ella. He feigned surprise.

'Are you offering me a bribe.' His eyes glittered.

'How dare you!' cried Ella. 'I thought that you were going to apologise for your insufferable behaviour yesterday.'

'I am sorry — with all my heart. It is because of my feelings towards you that I don't want to have to inform on you.'

'Or?' repeated Ella. He shrugged.

'That will be up to you. I'm sure we can work it out. It will mean only a little sacrifice. After all, we are becoming very good friends. I prom-

ise you will enjoy the experience.'
That was enough for Ella.

'I think it would be Costas and
Loukas' friendship I would be losing
if I agreed to your nasty little plan.
As well as my self-esteem!'

'Remember you have many good
friends in the village, Ella.'

'Well, if they are like you, I can do
without them,' she replied.

'They could be persuaded that you
are not a suitable person to teach
their children,' he said. Ella was
shocked that not only was he threatening her that he would have Loukas
prosecuted, but that he would turn
the whole village against her and she
would lose her job, unless she slept
with him. It was monstrous! They
regarded each other.

'Take a while to think about it, Ella,

but please believe me I do not wish us to lose our friendship over this.' For a moment, Ella was lost for words, but they were on their way . . . Then the door opened.

'Sorry, but it's rather hot in here. Shall I close the shutters?' June asked. She went over and fiddled about the window sill. Ella was already on her feet.

'Takis is just leaving, June.'

'Unwillingly,' he said, pushing in his chair with a meaningful glance at Ella.

'He has no time for coffee then,' replied June in the sickly-sweet voice she reserved for people she didn't like. 'I'll take off the kettle.' He looked from Ella to June, a sarcastic smile on his face.

'As I said, think over my proposition, Ella. By the way, the fires are approaching,' he said. 'I'd advise you both to think about collecting your valuables together. You are lucky, as the rest of us will be fire-fighting.'

'You're volunteering then?' sneered June.

'I shall be organising the evacuation of the village, if needed,' he replied.

'You mean, you're not getting your hands dirty. Now I'd be pleased if you'd leave.' She opened him the door.

'Please think over what I have said, Ella.' He was *still* trying. 'I only have your interests at heart.' She didn't answer. She felt as near to slapping Takis as she ever had anyone. But she had never been the victim of blackmail before.

Inside, she was worried. She knew

how powerful he was in the village. People were afraid of him. She was scared for herself, knowing a bad reference from the school might jeopardise her chances job wise, but more than that, she was for Loukas. What had this man got against him? Maybe it was a family feud? She couldn't do anything about that. But school matters were different. There must be some loophole! How she wished that June had been listening to the conversation.

After he had gone, Ella cried, 'Odious man! I wish you'd heard what he said.' To her surprise, June was grinning.

'Don't worry. Ella. I have it all in hand.'

'What do you mean. Were you listening at the door?'

'Come back through,' said June, indicating the dining room. Ella followed and watched June go over to the window sill. A moment later, she produced a small memo tape recorder. Ella stared. 'I got it all. Every word. And you thought I wasn't a techie. I'm not really. I used to use this when I did some secretarial work for Dimitri. I'm glad I didn't throw it away. I keep it in the dining room.'

'June, you're a treasure.' Ella hugged her friend instinctively. 'You know what he wanted from me, don't you?'

'Don't I just. This will settle him once and for all, and I know a few people who'll be very happy when it becomes common knowledge. Threatening *you*.' June gazed at the small machine as if it was its fault.

'He was trying to frighten us when he mentioned the fires, but everyone says they won't be allowed to get this far.' Then she looked at the dining room clock. 'Now hurry up. You've a date.'

'What would I do without you?' asked Ella.

'Not hear all the gossip?' June smiled.

It seemed hotter than ever as Ella drove off. In the mirror, she could see June waving and knew her friend was still anxious even though she was trying to cover the fact. But Ella would keep her promise and turn round if there was any danger.

Driving along, she noted that everything appeared to be quite normal with people going about their business as usual. The centre of Rhodes Town would be crowded so she decided to take the back road. That area never failed to surprise her. It was a conglomeration of small holiday hotels, each with their own pools and balconies which at night were adorned with swinging fairy lights. It also seemed to be an almost forgotten place with tiny tavernas, which lured their customers into the deep darkness of their cavernous interiors. A few children were walking along the winding road carrying nets and buckets, several dogs barked at her and dark men watched her drive by as they lounged against vine-covered lintels.

But soon the road opened up, snaking its narrow way towards the highway, off which she turned on the road to the mountains. She looked to see if she could see any sign of the fires, clouding the top of a neighbouring mountain and drifting down into the nearest valley. Nothing. But at one point she thought she could smell burning in the air. I'm imagining it, she thought.

She had to admit she was a bit nervous and wondered what her mother would have said if she had known what Ella was up to. She would have been shocked. Her idea of a proper daughter was someone who'd go shopping and chat about trivialities, who would enjoy parties and dress up at the slightest opportunity and could make small talk with others like her. What would she think of Loukas?

The trees' cooling shade was refreshing. Once again she thought how beautiful the island was. The idea of a fire eating it up made her shudder. She drove slowly and carefully into the first hairpin, preparing herself for any mad local driver. Since her accident, it had become a fear that one would race down and push her over the edge into the chasm of green below. She leaned to the side a little as she turned the wheel. Going up made her feel a little dizzy and it took some getting used to. How they drive buses up here, I'll never know, she thought. It must be bad for the passengers, never mind the drivers.

It was at that moment she caught a whiff of the acrid smell again and worried a little because she was sure she could smell burning. Perhaps it was Hermie's engine under stress?

The last car she'd driven in Britain was almost new and air conditioned. Not so, her little motor! She had to drive with windows open on the passenger and the driver's side, if she needed to breathe. There was no temperature on the dashboard either, but Ella estimated that outside it was at least 30 degrees. She was sweating now where the trees opened out, not lining the road any more as she drove higher. Instead they stood tall and sparse on the tinder dry ground.

About half way up, she brought the car to a halt at one of the stopping places. She'd told June she would be careful and she meant it. She got out and sniffed the air, looking first all around the car, then down at the road below, half-hidden by the dark greenery that partially masked it.

Then she realised she *could* smell fire! And it wasn't Hermie. But, as far as the eye could see, everything seemed normal.

In the distance, she glimpsed a hint of blue sea, which made her feel better, which she supposed was quite irrational. After all, she hadn't far to go now, then she would check again. She waited, arguing with herself. Was she being sensible? Maybe she *should* go back now, but — maybe she was imagining it was worse than it was and getting het up about nothing. Somewhere above she could hear the drone of an engine. She listened intently. A low aeroplane making for the airport or — a helicopter? The knowledge that she was not alone in that great green space cheered her. Not that they were nearby, but they represented civilisation.

How stupid I'm getting, she thought. You can see everything's all right. It's only a few minutes ago that I looked at the other mountain and it was fine. Returning to the car, Ella made her way up higher. Soon I shall see the house, she thought. The journey there seemed to have been the longest she'd ever driven — and so high! She found herself praying that he was waiting for her and began to rehearse what she should say to him.

Her hair was beginning to be blown around and she realised the wind was getting up. Then she could see the house through the trees, comforting her with its sturdy stone walls, but nearer, she could see no truck outside. The safe feeling dissipated. She brought the car to a stop and looked at her watch. She was five minutes late, so he probably didn't get the message. I shouldn't have stopped, she thought.

She made up her mind to go down to the house and drove slowly as if to give him time to arrive. She sat there and brushed the hair back from her forehead, remembering how he'd done the same in that beautiful brief moment when they had stopped outside the villa; when they had become close — until they broke apart. It all seemed a very long time ago.

She was lost in her own thoughts, but when she came to, she gasped! She couldn't see the road above. Smoke! The fire must have spread. Why had she been such an idiot as to go on. But she had seen nothing suspicious. *But you smelled it,* the little voice inside her head taunted. *You should have gone home. That's why he hasn't come.*

Ella had always been in control of her situation, but now she panicked. Below her was the mountain and the fire was coming towards her. What should she do? She jumped out of the car. Then looked at the shuttered house, her brain computing any means of escape. If she'd have been able to get in, it would have been no use. She's seen reports of so many fires over the years and how people had to evacuate their homes. She didn't want to think about those who had stayed to fight it from destroying their belongings and their livelihood.

'I have to find some way of getting down,' cried Ella out loud. *But you don't know the way down — if there is one.* The little voice insisted. *You're trapped.* Sheer drop on one side, fire on the other. It was a nightmare. Now, she couldn't see the road for smoke and somewhere above the helicopter was buzzing. But she was sure nobody could see her. Leaving the car, she rushed to the side of the house, her brain still trying to find a way of escape. She saw some buckets and ran over. They were full of water.

Taking one, she tipped it all over herself. She spluttered as it soaked through her light trousers and under-wear. She had no idea what else to do, but she thought it might help. Running behind the house, she stood and gasped at the height of the drop. The view that had been so beautiful, was now horrific, while the acrid smell of the smoke was choking her as the fire got nearer. At that moment, she thought she was finished.

Sweat mingled with her soaking clothes and her head whirled. If the fire got as far as her, she'd jump! At least she wouldn't burn to death. She could hardly see anything now as the smoke was thick. She took a deep breath, trying to make up her mind and then she heard a shout . . .

'Ella! Ella! Where are you?'

'Thank God,' she cried. 'Loukas!'

'Stay there!' he commanded. Fighting against the impulse to run towards him, she forced herself not to move. Seconds later, he was by her side, an unrecognisable figure. A scarf round his mouth and helmeted. She wanted to throw herself into his arms and sob, but he dragged her with him nearer to the drop. 'You stubborn little fool,' he said. She could only see his eyes. 'Did you think I wouldn't come?' He unwound a rope which was coiled across his body. 'Here!' He thrust the end of the rope into her hand. 'Now turn round and get behind me as though you were climbing on my back. Right. Now. Lash it round your waist and mine.' She did her best, with him helping her. 'Give me the end.' She gasped as it tightened and she knew he was knotting it. 'How do you feel?'

'All right.'

'No, are you secure?'

'Yes.'

'Then hang on to my shoulder straps and pray. We're going over. Down there we have a chance. Close your eyes — and don't open them!'

She grasped the belt that crisscrossed his back and hung on. The protective clothing he was wearing pressed against her breasts and hurt. She closed her eyes, ready to jump. Now he was here it didn't seem to matter. Now they were together. It was better than dying alone! They turned, with her, piggyback. She must be going over first. She shuddered and waited to fall.

She expected to feel a rush of air, but instead her body lurched backwards and she could feel space between hers and his, then a jerk, then another. She realised Loukas was climbing down the mountainside. She could hear him breathing heavily and prayed that he wouldn't lose his footing. *How strong was he?* She could smell the smoke on his clothes. It was in her mouth. She was struggling for breath because of it, or in panic.

In what seemed ages later, they stopped. She blinked. 'Don't look down!' he ordered.

'I won't,' she squeaked. She was crying.

'Don't worry. I'm only resting,' he said. 'We're on a ledge. I hunt on this mountain. I do this all the time. Okay?'

'Yes.' Sense was replacing panic now. 'I'm fine,' but her teeth were chattering.

'Great. If we can make the bottom, the fire will stay on the top. There's nowhere for it to go.'

She wanted to ask him if he could go on, but she kept quiet. The last thing he wanted now was questions. 'We're going to hit a path soon,' he said. 'Are you sure you're all right?'

'Yes.' She trusted him.

'We'll be okay. Off again.' She swallowed back her fear. She thought she might be sick at one point. At another, that she might let go of the straps and pull them both down, but Ella's will to live was stronger than she'd ever imagined. No one could imagine being in this situation, she told herself. Roped to a fireman, who was climbing down the mountain with you on his back. It was superhuman. This time, their progress seemed faster like when you've been on a journey and home is in sight.

Ella thought of his lovely house, which the fire couldn't have spared. What would he do? Where would he go? And Costas? Was he all right? He must have been as Loukas would never have left him. He was probably with his aunt now on the way to safety. Then she felt them lurch to a stop.

'At last! The path. You can open your eyes now.' The first thing she did was to glance over his shoulder and up. The little she could see without cricking her neck made her feel sick again. Could they possibly have come down that? It was sheer, except for a few stunted trees clinging to its grim, dark face. How had he managed it? He couldn't have done it often as he said.

'Shall I get off now?' she murmured into his back feeling guilty about how stupid she'd been putting them both in danger — and how he'd saved her life *again.*

'Not yet. Not in those shoes

anyway.' He must have been looking at her feet, wound round his waist. She oughtn't to have driven the car in flip-flops! He must think I'm useless, she thought.

'Thank you.' It was all she felt she could say.

She bumped up and down again as they descended. The path was very steep and scattered with huge stones. Ella realised it could have been a stream bed in the winter, trickling down from the mountain. He was right; she couldn't have managed it in such silly shoes. More trees were appearing now, clinging to the shale. Ella's effort with the bucket of water had made her clothes stiff against her skin and the pressure of his back against her must have bruised her, as her chest hurt a lot. She felt all in and she couldn't even imagine how *he* did, carrying her.

All the time, they must have been getting nearer to the road and she wished for the hundredth time that she'd been wiser to stay on it. But then . . . Loukas wouldn't have found her. She told herself off for being both unfair and irrational.

'I think you can get off now,' he said, 'but don't fall over when you do. You're bound to be shaky. Here will do.' They were in a small, grassy open space. 'I'll untie the rope.' She groaned as he unwound it, and his advice has been good, because she almost fell off, collapsing on to the grass.

A moment later he was tearing off the scarf around his face, then he fell down on the grass as well and lay in a crumpled heap. 'Loukas!' she cried. 'Are you all right?' She crawled over to him and she saw his eyes closed. 'Are you okay,' she repeated. His breath was shallow. She glanced round. What was she going to do? Was he unconscious? She looked down at him and his eyes opened,

'Good thing you aren't any heavier,' he said and closed them again. She breathed a sigh of relief and lay beside him without speaking. Then, seconds later, he sat up and wiped the sweat off his face. 'What the hell do you think you were doing, putting our lives at risk?'

'I — I . . .' she began.

'For a schoolteacher, you are really stupid.'

'I'm sorry,' she said. 'You've every right to be angry and I have no excuse except . . . '

'I don't want to know,' he replied, and lay down again. She waited. 'Just getting my wind back,' he muttered. She still didn't say anything, but she was thinking about how he'd treated her when she'd crashed the car. It's his way of coping with it, I suppose, she thought. And he's right about me being stupid. But will he forgive me? The episode with Takis came into her mind, but she crushed the thought.

'Come here!' His voice was gruff. She was facing him.

'For God's sake, don't you ever do what you're told?' He opened his arms and she came to him and put her wet head in the crook of his shoulder, not knowing whether to cry or laugh. The next few moments felt so right that she didn't want to move, but soon, he stirred. Then he got up and she followed. He looked up to the sky. 'Can you hear that chopper? Hopefully they'll spot us soon.'

'I think so.' Now she could.

'There's the road,' he said, pointing. 'Can you make it?' She nodded. 'Then come on. We need to be out in the open.' Both breathing heavily from the exertion, they scrambled down on to the road.

'Do you know what the chopper is doing?' he asked. She shook her head. 'Looking for idiots who happened to be wandering on the mountain oblivious of the fires.'

'Including me. I said I was sorry.'

'And so you should be.' He was looking down at her with a strange expression on his face, which was streaked with sooty dirt. 'I found you, because the chopper managed to spot your car and communicated with the men on the ground. I was one of them. I never thought you'd be silly enough to come up here.'

'*I know,*' she retorted, grimacing, 'but I'm too weary to fight with you now.'

'Who said I wanted a fight? All I — we, both need is for the chopper to see us. Come on!' They ran into the middle of the road. He saw her apprehensive look from left to right. 'No one will come. The road's blocked off.' The sound was louder. 'It's circling. Wave!' he ordered. Then the chopper was in sight. It turned away. 'It's okay, they've seen us. Now we have to wait.' He went back over to the side of the road and sat down. She followed, putting some distance between them.

'Won't it pick us up?'

'Nowhere to land.'

'What are we waiting for?'

'The men who have been blocking off the roads to stop *anyone* going up the mountain.' She couldn't decide whether he was getting at her again and she certainly wasn't going to say she'd seen them down below earlier on, nor that she thought they were workmen!

'They'll be here soon, I hope,' he added. A few minutes later, they could hear the sound of a heavy truck. Loukas got to his feet and she followed, wiping her hands down her dirty, smoke-blackened clothing. Loukas hailed in the vehicle and then spoke rapidly to the passenger, who got out. The man was wearing similar clothes to Loukas, who beckoned Ella. 'Get in.' He indicated the front seat.

'Where are you . . .'

'We'll be in the back. Don't argue.'

'I wasn't going to.' Feeling crestfallen and extremely foolish, Ella smiled weakly at the driver. Soon, as they cruised along, Ella felt her head nodding and whatever she did, she couldn't keep awake any longer.

The truck stopped with a jolt and a dazed and exhausted Ella could hardly remember where she was.

'Where are we?' she asked in English. The driver shrugged, but he was smiling. Then everything became clear. 'I've been asleep,' she said, half to herself. Of course, he couldn't understand. She looked out of the window. They were at June's. 'Thank you,' she said and the driver grinned and nodded.

The passenger door opened to a very dirty and grime-streaked Loukas. I must look like that, thought Ella. 'You're home,' he said. She was about to say goodbye, when he took her arm and helped her towards the gate. 'You look all in. Come on.'

Then the truck drove off. Ella's spirits soared. He wasn't going with them. 'Thank you, Loukas. I don't know what I'd have done if you hadn't found me.'

'You'd have been fried,' he said. She shuddered.

'What time is it?' Her watch had stopped. It must have been soaked by her efforts with the bucket.

'Late. We both could do with a good

sleep.' She felt a little throb inside, then told herself off for being so hopelessly romantic, even in this situation. He had his arm round her quite tightly supporting her as they made their way towards the villa. The nap in the truck hadn't done her much good and the perfume from June's fragrant shrubs was soporific.

The villa door opened. 'You're back,' cried June. 'I've been worried to death. It said on the news the fire had reached the mountain. And *you* saved her.' She embraced Loukas.

'I was only doing what I'm trained for,' he said, looking pleased.

'You and I know there's more to it than that,' replied June directly. 'What a mess you both look, but I'm not going to ask you a thing.' June had taken over. 'You go straight to the bathroom, Ella,' she ordered, and turning to Loukas, 'you can use the downstairs shower. I'll fetch more towels. Then I'll go and make the tea. Oh — tea for you, Loukas?'

'Anything wet,' he replied, with a smile, looking at Ella.

'Then a good rest I think before dinner. By the way, I have to go out tonight to see my friend. I'll be late so I'll lay the table and leave it.' She looked meaningfully at Ella. 'I'm sure you have things to discuss.'

When Ella woke it was almost dark — and she felt disappointed. She didn't know what she'd been expecting — but it hadn't happened. Then she told herself she was being selfish. She listened, then she could hear noises on the mezzanine. That's where he must be. It was small place between the two storeys of the main floors and an area where June used to put up the overspill of any friends who came to visit. A bed was always made up and it was extremely convenient. Although she didn't know Loukas that well, Ella had a feeling he preferred not causing trouble to people. She hoped he'd had a good sleep too. They couldn't have talked the way they were. She wondered whether she should get up in case . . . of she didn't know what.

She realised she had gone to sleep in her wrap, but she didn't feel like dressing. She thought about several of her friends back in London. Probably they'd have crept along to the mezzanine, but Ella knew that Loukas wouldn't be happy if she did.

Maybe he was still a "one-woman man." She hoped not.

She sat on the bed and wondered what to do next. Perhaps he was still asleep? Then her heart jumped as she heard a knock. 'June?' she asked, but then she remembered she'd gone out and that it must be Loukas.

'Ella. Are you awake?'

'Yes. Come in.'

He was wearing an old-fashioned dressing gown, but he looked like the old Loukas. Any clothes would have looked good on him and even this one couldn't hide his hard-muscled body. Besides it was much too short. 'I think it belonged to June's husband,' he said grimacing. She didn't laugh.

'Of course, you haven't any clothes,' she murmured.

'No, which is awkward. I'll have to put my old ones back on. But that doesn't matter now. I want to talk to you.' She could hardly breathe, thinking what might be coming. She patted the bed. 'Come here.' He sat down beside her. 'You look better,' he said.

'Thank you.'

'I've things to tell you, Ella' he added. 'June was right. Things I should have spoken about before . . .' He stopped.

'Before what?'

'Until . . .' he began. 'No, I mean . . .' She could see he was struggling. 'I told you, I'm hopeless with women!'

'You're not. Take it easy.' Here she was, telling a married man to take it easy! 'I'm listening.'

"The problem is — I don't trust women,' he said, looking straight at her. She hadn't expected that.

'Why? Do you think they're going to jump you?' She realised she'd done the wrong thing by making a joke.

His face was serious. 'I assume June hasn't told you that bit then?' Ella frowned. 'The big bit.' He sounded bitter.

'You mean — Xanthe. I can see why you feel like you do. It wasn't right that she died like that. I know you loved her very much.'

'Once,' he said.

'But you'll get over it eventually. I think I understand how you feel.' She thought how can I say these things when I have absolutely no idea. No experience. All she knew was that she wanted to comfort — to love him.

'You're sweet,' he said. 'But you can't understand.'

'Tell me then and I'll try.' She waited.

'Xanthe was everything to me.' His voice was low. 'I loved her since we were in our teens. Even at school. We met there, but she was the clever one. You know she was a teacher?' Ella nodded. 'Like you . . .' He broke off. 'But . . . when she died . . .' He looked at Ella and she held his gaze, then felt his hand slip into hers like he needed her support. She held it tightly. He sighed. '. . . I was — relieved when she died.' His eyes held hers. 'You think that's a terrible thing to say, don't you? I can see by your face. But it's the truth. Relieved,' he repeated as if she wasn't there. 'But not when I found her body — or what was left of it. Only afterwards.'

Ella was shocked. What did he mean relieved? How can you be *relieved* when someone you love dies? She held on to his hand as she felt him ready to withdraw his. 'Yes, I've felt guilty since, not only for her, but for Costas. You want to know why.'

'Yes, I do.'

'That night, Xanthe was leaving me. Leaving us both.'

'What?' She felt the perspiration bursting on her forehead. She felt relieved too, which couldn't be natural either.

'She'd had other affairs, but not on this island. It could have been my fault. I let her stay over there, because I thought she was working and I trusted her. When I found out, it broke me up inside. We had massive

252

rows, until I was sick of it. I wanted it all to end, but believe me, not like that. I do still have a heart! Sometimes I thought I'd do something terrible, then I remembered Costas depended on me. I wouldn't let her have him. She was a bad mother.

'I forgave her so many times. I suppose because I still loved her in a funny kind of way. Maybe it was pride. I didn't want anyone to know, but they all did. That's why they keep out of my way. Then she started an affair with someone here on the island right here under my nose. I would have killed him if I'd known what was happening. He was in the car with her and he walked away untouched. He got away with it. It's a wonder he did, because she was driving. He was *supposed* to be the innocent party. 'Loukas almost growled the last words. 'I hated him then and I still do.' He was breathing heavily.

'This is the first time,' he added, 'that I've been able to tell anyone these things and I have to pretend to Costas that his mother was a saint. I keep all her things, all her clothes, because I can't bring myself to tear them to pieces.' There were tears in his eyes. Ella put her arm around him and he leaned his head into her shoulder.

'I'm sorry,' he said, 'you don't want to hear all this. Besides, you have someone else?'

'You don't know how much I want to hear!' she replied. 'But there's no one.' He lifted his head and the tears were drying on his cheeks. "I know that it looked as if I had. But I feel nothing for the man. He put me in that position. I can't stand him.'

'That makes two of us,' he said.

'You mean . . . you mean the man . . . was *Takis?* Takis and Xanthe.' Her head whirled as it all made sense.

'Now you understand,' he said. 'When I saw you together, I flipped.'

'Oh, Loukas,' she cried, 'if only you could have explained before. I've been so sad.'

'I expect you hate *me* now,' he said. 'I know I'm a moody guy.'

'I don't care.' He put his hand forward and brushed back her hair.

'You are beautiful,' he said. 'I wanted to tell you about Xanthe before, but I was always afraid to open up.' He shrugged, then added,

'I suppose I thought Takis was going to take you too. He's everything I'm not. Good-looking, with women falling at his feet. Loads of money . . .' Ella put a finger to his lips.

'Shhh. If you were like him, I wouldn't be able to stand you either. I'm not on the look-out for a man like that. I'm looking for . . .' It was now or never. '. . . someone like you. But June said you were a 'one-woman man.' I thought that you loved Xanthe so much that you could never replace her. Now I know what she meant that you couldn't trust another woman. But you know you can trust me, don't you?'

'Yes. And June was right in a way. I didn't want anyone ever again until I met you. Costas loves you as well.'

'He's so sweet.' "As well" must have

meant that Loukas loved her!

'When I saw you with Takis, I wanted to tear his heart out.'

'Forget him. He can do what he likes with his job. And then I can teach Costas at home.'

'What do you mean?'

'Takis came here yesterday and he threatened me.' Ella was worried when she saw the grim look on Loukas' face.

'What did he do?' His voice was hard.

'He's determined to stop Costas going to school and to report you to the authorities. He said that he'd only withdraw his accusations if I . . .'

'*Tell me.*'

'If I slept with him,' she said. 'And if I didn't, I'd lose my job. He's very powerful. But I told him where to go.

Loukas, don't worry. Forget him even though he hates you as much as you hate him. He can't destroy us. June got the conversation on tape. We've trapped him. You don't have to do anything silly. I don't want you to get into any trouble. Please say something.' He took a deep breath as if trying to control himself and Ella could hardly bear the wait.

'Is I love you good enough?' His voice was strong as he took her in his arms. With those beautiful words resounding in her head, she felt her body melt into his as he kissed her in the way she'd dreamed he would. They lay against the pillows, entwined together, savouring each other's nearness.

'Yes, but one thing I don't understand is — why you let Anna work for you. She's Takis' cousin.'

'I'm sorry for her, that's all. She used to work for us and I hadn't the heart to let her go. She has a rough time of it at home. Do you mind?'

'Not now. Loukas,' she said, nestling against him, looking into his eyes as he smiled down at her. 'Do you think it burned down?'

'What?'

'Your house. It's such a lovely place.'

'It's still only a heap of stones, Ella,' he smiled. 'But if it's burned down and if you want, I'll build you another.' His dark eyes smouldered.

'Just as pretty?' She waited breathlessly for what she knew was coming.

'Prettier,' he replied, holding her tightly. 'Costas and I, we'll be the happiest men in the world, if you will come and live with us in our house on the mountain? Will you, Ella?'

'I will,' she replied, knowing that she would never be more sure of anything in her whole life.

We hope you have enjoyed this Large Print book. Other Thorndike, Wheeler, Kennebec, and Chivers Press Large Print books are available at your library or directly from the publishers.

For information about current and upcoming titles, please call or write, without obligation, to:

Publisher
Thorndike Press
10 Water St., Suite 310
Waterville, ME 04901
Tel. (800) 223-1244

or visit our Web site at:

http://gale.cengage.com/thorndike

OR

Chivers Large Print
published by AudioGO Ltd
St James House, The Square
Lower Bristol Road
Bath BA2 3SB
England
Tel. +44(0) 800 136919
email: info@audiogo.co.uk
www.audiogo.co.uk

All our Large Print titles are designed for easy reading, and all our books are made to last.